AGAINST MY WINDOW

JAMESON FAMILY SERIES BOOK 3

TRACEE LYDIA GARNER

GARNER SOLUTIONS, LLC

Against My Window

© Copyright 2021 by Tracee Lydia Garner

www.Traceegarner.com

Published by Tracee Lydia Garner

ISBN: 978-0-9981099-3-0

Formatting by Tracee Lydia Garner

© Editing by Best Words Editing

© Cover Design by Ally Hastings

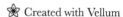 Created with Vellum

ALSO BY TRACEE LYDIA GARNER

FICTION

Family Affairs (All That & Then Some anthology)

PARKER BROTHERS FAMILY SERIES

Anchored Hearts (Book 1 | Cole Parker's Story)

Deadly Affections (Book 2 | Dexter Parker's Story)

Fatal Opposition (Book 3 | James Parker's Story)

JAMESON FAMILY SERIES

Whatever May Come

Jameson Family Book 1

A Current Affair | (Dean's story)

Jameson Family Book 2

Against My Window | (Jina's story)

Jameson Family Book 3

Occasional Hero | (Jojo's story) COMING SOON

Jameson Family Book 4

ALSO BY TRACEE LYDIA GARNER

NONFICTION

Pack Light: Thoughts for the Journey

COMING SOON

Disability: A Field Guide for the Rest of Us

ACKNOWLEDGMENTS

To God be the Glory.

1

By the time Jina Jameson-King arrived at the hospital, she'd been through the entire dizzying gamut of emotions. When she'd heard about the accident, she'd been in such a rush to get there that all had been a blur until she found herself sitting in the hospital's garage, by which time the initial rush had cooled to let in some common sense. She sat there, taking time to remember past affronts, feeling the anger creep back in to replace the panic and concern she had initially felt.

No, of course she didn't want Tony dead, and naturally she cared; but she was so done with it all. The last time she was there she'd also had to say goodbye to her infant son. The sense of loyalty by which she had been driven to come back had quickly been replaced by raw pain: the kind that left an ache so deep that she thought she might throw up, for the second time that day. The first time, earlier that morning, hadn't been related to any of this, because she hadn't yet received the devastating phone call. She couldn't deal with that. All she could do now was to continue praying.

But she was there now, in that hot and humid afternoon. Three months ago, she'd made the same trek through the

INova parking garage with her baby in her arms - before she'd left without him. She couldn't stand it. She couldn't be here. She texted Jojo. He was the only one that she would bother about the burdens she carried.

The room was eerily quiet outside the curtain, where she waited patiently to see what was going on.

"I'm sorry Ma'am, have you been helped?"

"Um, I'm uh, Jina Jameson. A Mr. King was brought in from a car accident." She didn't recognize her own voice as it came out, but so much had happened to her in the last year that she found herself slowly shrinking into someone else entirely: a shell of her former self. No more fight left.

"Yes, I'll get the doctor. Your husband is just coming up from the anesthesia, ma'am. His surgery went well and it's a miracle…"

She breathed a sigh of relief. He'd be fine. She was sad but relieved: he wouldn't need her, he'd be fine. She shouldn't've said anything at all to him. Instead, like the coward she seemed to be becoming, she should have simply picked up the phone and called him. *Wow, heartless – at least when he broke up with you, he did it to your face.*

Well, so what, she thought - that was still incredibly painful. *But I thought you didn't believe him?* a voice whispered.

"I didn't," she whispered back harshly - then threw up her hands. *Great, now I'm having a full-blown conversation with myself,* she thought wryly. *What's next: talking about myself in the third person?*

She wondered wistfully if she could've just called the hospital from the garage rather than actually going in. Anything to remove herself… *Like a cowardly lion,* continued her thoughts. *Sure, just call him on the phone and be like hey, how you doin'? Like Wendy Williams. Then drop a 'glad you're okay' and flee.*

Jina's cheeks heated and she kept her eyes on the speckled hospital floor. Yes, she and Tony had been together less than two months ago; but it wasn't anything, she told herself - even though she knew otherwise.

She banished her painful unbidden thoughts before straightening as the doctor emerged and turned to her. She looked up at him, hoping an optimistic greeting left her lips. "Hello, doctor?"

The doctor smiled reassuringly at her. "How are you, Mrs. King?"

"Jameson – it's Ms. Jameson," Jina said, keeping her voice low but firm.

"Oh? Okay, well then…"

The curtain swung open and she couldn't resist glancing in before it swung back into place. Her heart sped up from the sight of him lying there: immobile, unconscious - just so painfully still. Before she could protest, the doctor ushered her closer to the bed, just a few feet away from him, and she went kind of deaf. The doctor quickly pulled up a chair and she sank into it, not able to take her eyes off him.

"Why - why is his face so swollen?"

The figure before her didn't look like Tony at all. She loved his face: his dark eyes and chiseled features. The man lying before her looked like he'd been in a fight with Mike Tyson before being tossed to George Foreman in the same ring. No matter what the two of them had been through, she hated to see him like that.

"We had to repair his back," the doctor replied gently. "He had extensive damage to it - so much that he could have been paralyzed. Once the swelling is down, though, he will be okay, even if he'll have some chronic pain issues, but he should make a full recovery."

Jina nodded absently. She had no idea what to do next. At least the shock had lessened now. She stood again and placed her hand on the railing. He was eerily still. She was aware of voices talking elsewhere, but she was not really listening. She was mesmerized by the silent, bandaged man lying on the on the bed.

"Memory loss."

"What?" She looked up sharply, shutting off her phone. She crossed her arms tightly over her chest, against the chill in the room but also against the feelings she kept telling herself that she no longer held for him. Surely this was no kind of love? Even if it was, she resolved that no one other than her mother and siblings would ever know. Would *he* know? If memory loss was a possibility, would he even remember that they weren't together any longer: that there had been something that had strained their relationship and eventually broken it?

When she'd met Anthony King, she thought she would never trust anyone again. Ever. Then it was a classic story of being won over by his charming smile, eyes so huge she felt like she was drowning in them, and lashes that no woman could match no matter how much product she used.

"He has been asking for you," the doctor added.

She just smiled tightly in response. Now that he was awake, his eyes searched for something. And Jina grew annoyed that all of this was because of the souvenir, a racy little sports car his father had bought for him to woo him back into their dysfunctional relationship, and years of abandonment.

"So uh, it's been in the news that you two are recently estranged," the doctor continued. "He will find out about that, of course, but I think it's best if..."

"If I lie?" She obviously watched too many movies.

The doctor laughed. "No, Mrs. King - "

"Jameson," she corrected quickly. She glanced at Tony. *So what?* He had no way of knowing she hadn't ever actually completed the divorce paperwork after it was written up and served to her. Neither did this doctor, for that matter.

At last, Tony spoke to her from the bed. "Look, could you

just come a little closer?" His hand reached out to touch hers. The tension in her eased a little. She knew that she still had feelings for him: that was part of why she did not want to be there. It wasn't like she had any time to review the situation, be angry, curse him out or let go of the feelings she had for him. This entire scene was new to her: uncharted territory. She had no idea how to feel, and she needed the time and the energy to figure that out.

When another woman breezed into the room, Jina's hand snapped away. Sheila King, Tony's stepmother, came into complete focus, but her very pungent perfume permeated the room, first causing Jina to wrinkle her nose, not just from the new smell but the woman herself.

"Darling, my God, what has happened to you?" the woman exclaimed, looking at Tony before taking in the rest of the room. "Oh, oh, uh, Jina," the woman gritted out tersely.

Jina rolled her eyes. At least she'd been acknowledged this time. Throughout their marriage, things hadn't exactly been cordial between the two women. In fact, Jina found herself wondering why Sheila chose to acknowledge her now.

Tony evidently hadn't even noticed Sheila come in. He was still looking at Jina.

"Honey, I'm here." His stepmother tapped his other arm impatiently and he flinched.

"My heart tells me something is amiss here, and that we have an awkward relationship."

"Oh, yes, we did have a very troubled start my dear, but I've made amends! We're past that now,"

"Is that true, Jina?"

"What? Uh, I don't know."

"You do know."

"No, I – uh…"

"Well, for heaven's sake - even in this comprised state, he still seeks you for everything!" his mother exploded. "That's why your marriage - that's why your marriage is broken, don't you see? You're your own man, you don't need her."

Jina looked away. "I gotta go."

"Please don't leave," Tony pleaded.

She wanted to tell him she'd come back, but what on earth for? They were simply using diversionary tactics to avoid the inevitable. He'd had those divorce papers served to her not long ago. Sure, he'd forgotten now, but whenever it came back, it would be that much more difficult to do.

"Tony, I can't help you, I'm sorry." *I have my own issues,* she thought to herself. "I know you and I are... going through some troubled times, so it would be best for you to leave this alone and focus on getting better."

"But we're not married - what's she talking about?" Tony responded, dazed.

Lost in her own thoughts, Jina's head snapped up. She wanted to be angry, but the moment she looked at Tony's confused face, everything that has transpired in the last week came flooding back to her.

"We're getting a divorce, Tony," she said softly. "Thank you for reminding us, Sheila - you're too gracious," she added sarcastically.

"Well it's important he know the truth," Sheila said smugly.

"Get out."

Though her head was bowed, she heard Tony loud and clear. Although Sheila was looking at her in triumph, Tony spoke again.

"I said get out. Leave. Let me talk to her by myself. Please?"

"But, but - "

"Out!" Tony exclaimed.

Jina just stood there. His tone had startled even her. Despite what sounded like confirmation that the divorce was a mistake - and it obviously said something about how he viewed her - Jina's mind refused to believe it. Elation and grief warred within her brain, but she kept a watchful eye on Sheila, who seemed to take several audible breaths, looking at Tony in silent pleading before she eventually stood and, bristling all the way, finally left the two of them alone.

Jina wanted to follow her out, but didn't. Not yet. Tony's eyes returned to her.

"Jina, tell me the truth, please."

"It is the truth," she said quickly. She wasn't angry, just annoyed.

She looked toward the door, wondering if the poisonous Sheila might be standing on the other side, listening, ready to pounce - or worse, ready to confront Jina when she left. She grabbed her purse, sorry she'd even come.

"Well, why?" Tony said.

"I don't know, okay? I don't know."

It took every ounce of her resilience not to leave, but when the silence grew and he sat before her looking so confused, she knew she had to go. She was reassured that Tony had told Sheila to leave, for once; but it didn't solve their most pressing problems. Their marriage was still broken. She exited the room, almost running from the building. She let her tears fall then, glad that both her children still had a father: the one currently staying with her sister, and the one growing in her belly.

2

When she got to the parking lot, she felt like she could breathe again at last. Hospitals made her sick. Despite whatever had just happened back there, she knew she probably hadn't seen nor heard the last of him. Something told her she wouldn't get rid of him that easily.

"So, how's he look?" intoned a deep male voice she recognized.

Jina jumped. She'd know her brother Jojo's voice anywhere, but she was annoyed that perhaps she was so distracted that she hadn't been paying as much attention to her surroundings as she should have. She didn't even know if he'd been standing there the whole time or whether he'd just got out of his truck. In her defense, he was a career military man who seemed to move like a sniper... Nonetheless, she was annoyed and anxious that she had clearly been so preoccupied during the lengthy walk from the hospital exit to her car. She eyed him, newly wary of everything in her messed-up, suddenly-complicated life.

"Jina, baby girl?"

"Yes, what?" she snapped, more angrily than she intended. She counted to ten, knowing that if she was indeed having a relapse her brother would tell the rest of her siblings, who would tell their respective spouses, who would also tell her mother – and poof, off to Tish's she'd likely be cajoled into going. At least there'd be one good thing to come of such a trip: she'd get to see her Robby.

She wanted to make that decision on her own, though. In fact, at this moment she had half a mind to order her plane ticket herself; but she had held off so far. They'd surely be worried if she hit that panic button of her own accord.

"I sent you a text so you'd know I'd be out here," her brother said.

"Okay, thanks - thanks for coming," she sighed. "All isn't well, but I'm dealing. Oh, and I appreciate your text, but, um, sorry, I didn't check my messages while I was in there. Anyway, yeah, he looks banged up, but he's going to be fine. A little head trauma, but he'll live."

"But he's got some memory loss?" Jojo said.

"I'm sorry, if you know these things why do you ask me?" Jina returned hotly.

"It helps me see what kind of mood you're in," he replied with a twinkle.

"Well, have you gotten enough short and highly charged answers yet to make your assessment?"

"Oh yeah, I got it, but more so from the body language though than the verbiage, for sure," he laughed.

Jina laughed too then, in spite of herself. She loved her brother: he was the only one of her siblings who let her be mean to him. Their relationship was close: when she was mad, he knew not to mess with her too much, but she knew she could count on him no matter what. After a parting hug, she drove away.

Right then, she didn't have anywhere to be. At this

moment, no-one needed her. Certainly not her husband, whatever he remembered. Nothing had changed. They were still on a course to split, despite whatever was going on with his memory. Who knew: it might all come crashing back to him, and who would get the brunt of that? Her. Left once again to piece her life back together after his, his... She couldn't even bring herself to think about it long enough to name it.

It made everything hurt, especially her heart; not to mention the sadness she felt as she wiped her face, trying to grasp the steering wheel with tear-slick hands. She slowed up on the street. She noticed that all of a sudden she wasn't far from one of her homes. She hadn't meant to drive here, but this wasn't the first time her desire for the comforts of home had steered her there on autopilot.

She thought about her conversation with her brother. She knew he didn't believe what she had done, but the truth was that a lot had taken its toll on her, causing her to make really horrible decisions. The worst decision had been asking her sister to take her child for a few days.

She felt alone and disgusted with herself, but she felt somewhat justified too. There was so much love in her sister's house. Robby was there with her sister, her mother, ten-year-old Thomas, not to mention the twins, almost a year now. He was having a good time, she was sure. "Mommy is coming back, honey," she whispered, praying that he'd want to come with her: that a few days didn't mean that much to a child. She was probably wrong, she thought dejectedly.

Jina walked slowly up to the door of her old house. Her entire family had lived under this one roof until she and Jojo went to college, then Tish left too. After that, their father had been diagnosed with Alzheimer's, which had brought all of them back less than a year ago to take their turns caring for him. Their mother remained by her husband's side at all times, and Dean had stayed most nights, with Chyna, Dean's now wife, pitching in too, and becoming their father's caregiver.

Jina took a deep breath. So much time had passed, but it didn't seem like any time at all. All the pain just felt raw and tender: still a fresh wound.

Despite all her guilt about Robby, she was comforted by the presence of her sister and Mother. She knew they could give her little boy everything he needed and more right then, and would do for the foreseeable future. She had to believe that, or she'd go even crazier.

No one understood her decision and Jojo was right, it was only to be for a few days; but slowly yet surely, as he'd painfully reminded her, those few days had slid into a second week. *Well, when you give away all of your responsibilities, I guess you can lollygag all you want to, now can't you?*

She shook away the bitter thought as she took in the house's familiar exterior. Everything Dean had done to it was beyond perfection. The pressure wash, the fresh coat of gray paint coating the old brick, the new awning and fresh shutters restored its timeless appeal. She just loved looking at it. He'd done most of it himself, later outsourcing the bigger jobs to finish up the house as soon as he and Chyna had married.

Distractedly punching in the code, she turned the handle - only for it not to budge. Applying more concentration, she looked at each of the numbers and used her index finger to enter each number more carefully. Nothing. She let out an exasperated breath and kicked the door in frustration, instantly hoping she hadn't marred the paint job. She walked around to the back, passing her mother's rarely-driven Honda SUV sitting in the driveway. She approached the fence - even that was new - hoping the gate wasn't locked too. All these precautions had Dean's touch all over them. Yes, she remembered now: he and Chyna were going to be gone to Africa for their honeymoon for a month to find their new life path, or whatever middle-aged people did when they had plenty of money. She knew all this extra security was only an effort to keep out the bad guys - and he and Chyna had seen enough bad guys to last them forever. She herself hadhad a hand in ensuring her brother and Chyna, Jina's best friend, hadn't been implicated in any wrongdoing. She loved them, all of her family, and would do anything for them – even though this stance had cost her dearly over the years. But she couldn't deal with conjuring all that up - not right then, in any case. She had enough to contend with in the present. The fence wasn't going to be kind either...

She paused. Why was she even there? There was nothing she wanted in the house, except for the simple comforting feeling of being in her mother's room, smelling her familiar smells. Taking a nap somewhere no one would bother her was deeply enticing at that moment. She had only been out in the heat for twenty minutes. Frustrated, she gave the fence's gate a kick - and, to her surprise, it gave way.

She went through it and tried to close it behind her, but her kick had bent the little latch - she made a mental note to fix it later. The neighborhood didn't have a high crime rate, but the Jameson family had had their fair share of nut jobs in the past. Thankfully, they'd all been put away or died, she thought to herself, recalling Dean and Chyna's most recent brush with danger. No one had been in the house for several months now, and the latest security change meant that even she wasn't getting in - and she belonged there.

"How about that?" she muttered to the air. "Can't get into my own darn house." She laughed shortly. It was becoming pretty clear that she didn't actually belong anywhere. She felt like a ship without a sail, just drifting further and further away from everyone and everything she had once held in her heart and in her arms.

In spite of all her dark thoughts, it really was a beautiful day. Summer was her favorite season: although the heat did get a mite oppressive in July, it was time for fun, for picnics and fairs and fireworks. She remembered all the vacations and excursions with Tony. It was hard to imagine doing that with just Robby for company. She'd lost herself somewhere along the way: she had spent a ton of time planning for a baby, only to produce no baby. She'd had three miscarriages, then a great job as Editor in Chief for the longest-running newspaper in the country, and, finally, one precious baby. Now she was left with a husband that had just almost died and one impending divorce. She was just missing a partridge in a pear tree. It felt like her life had been just one bad decision after another, and now here she was on her mother's back porch, lost in an abyss of nothingness. The sun beat down on her back as she hung her head low and surveyed the property.

The last time she'd been there for any length of time was for Chyna and Dean's wedding. Dean had worked so hard to surprise Chyna with the beautiful ceremony that Jina had helped with, but had also almost ruined by spilling the beans. She had just been so excited that they were finally getting together after all those years. Now she gazed out over the wide stretches of overgrown grass, the small red tricycle in the back, the recently-painted blue shed looking brand new in the daytime sun. There was even a deep red picnic table and benches Dean had built from reclaimed wood: extra-long, to accommodate their growing families.

Everywhere her eyes landed, Jina recalled something from her childhood. She wondered why she kept going back there, when it was torture every time. Maybe it was some sort of fortification she sought. Every couple that had lived in the house over the years was either still together or at peace: though her father had passed, he'd lived out his days there. Joe Senior and her Mom had often sat out on that very porch, looking out over the fruits of their labor - their children, godchildren, grandchildren – with simple contentment and longevity.

Scooting up to the top step, Jina lay back. The awkward

position felt like something a chiropractor might order. She felt like she should stretch her hands above her head and do some sort of backward-lying dog, or whatever the yoga term was. The wood was hard, yet the sun made her feel cocooned, easing the tension from her bones as if she were in a lovely sauna. She felt so relaxed that she even wondered fleetingly whether she could give some meditation a try. She had tended to regard herself as too highly-strung for such holistic practices, when she usually felt like she got equivalent benefits out of a good old nap.

She did focus for a while, thanking God for saving Tony and her mind once more. Silently, she asked the good Lord to help her put the pieces of her life back together, even if that meant flying solo. She listened to the birds overhead, gradually quieting her mind. The skinny dogwood tree overhead provided just enough shade for her face, and she soon drifted into a light sleep.

It wasn't long before the panic returned: fear, rejection. She stirred, unable to properly wake up from her half-sleep state. How could she get back to the warmth, the protection and the net of safety that shielded her for all the years she'd known Tony? She'd been so certain he was the man for her, and believed she could trust him, only to receive a notice that said otherwise. That everything she believed was a sham.

"I've got you," she heard someone say - only it wasn't Tony. Tony wasn't there, and he hadn't been for some time. Wrapped up in his work like she herself used to be, before she lost everything. She turned away in her mind, recoiling from the thought that so much of this was her fault too. He could have talked to her, she reasoned: they could have worked it out. He didn't have to take such drastic action…

Squinting in the sun as she came to at last, she became aware that she was wrapped in the arms of a man. Not Tony, she reasoned blearily – it couldn't be - not so soon? She'd just left him at the hospital - he wouldn't be well so fast…

Catching the eyes of the man who held her, she scrambled away. His arms were solid, his chest broad –

She woke with a start. Leaping to her feet, disoriented, she lost her balance and tumbled down the three porch steps to the patio below.

3

When her eyes opened, she was startled to see a figure towering over her. She shielded her eyes to get a good look at him, as if that was necessary: the strength of his cologne announced his presence very effectively. Even the mosquitos around him were probably dying a slow death of asphyxiation.

She hauled herself to her feet, registering her own scraped-up hand from the fall. What was scarier was the look of triumph on the man's face. Instead of seeing if she was OK, helping her up even, he just stared at her – like always.

"Jina, hey, I uh - you were flailing a bit in your sleep and when I saw you were crying, I just thought I shouldn't leave you by yourself. I mean, why aren't you inside? Did you fall asleep out here on purpose?"

"No – well, this is my house, but..."

Jina stopped talking as she noted his cynical expression. She reviewed what she had just said. It was completely believable - wasn't it? Now, was it the truth? No, but he didn't know that. She started again, trying to muster confidence.

"This is my house, Keith," she said firmly. "I just came out to enjoy my backyard."

Why she bothered with this charade she didn't know. It wasn't her house per se, but as long as she was a part of the family, she had a rightful claim to being around it, at least. In any case, she really couldn't stand Keith Munroe. Just another one of her husband's stupid long-time friends, who always seemed to pop up at the worst times.

Jina took a deep breath and brushed the specks of blood off her hands. She gave him an irate look and stomped off back around to her car. She hoped to get some tissues and then proceed to drive far, far away. She shouldn't have come there at all. Mental note: next time, she needed to text Dean for the code - or probably Jojo, since Dean was in Africa. She tried not to let it hurt, being shut out, being rejected. It was a painful reminder that she was always being left out somewhere - even left out of her own marriage. *And yet you send your own son away, the one God gave to you.* Jina took a breath, fighting to keep her anxiety down. The guilt over that was just as stifling.

She was sitting in the car when Keith appeared at the passenger window. She frowned: it was a nice day and she'd left the windows down.

"Jina, you gotta stop being so angry."

"I'm sorry, um, who said I was angry?" she snapped.

"Well, I'm trying to have a conversation with you, but you're in a huff, you're looking at me cross-eyed, short lipped. I'm worried about you, and I just spent the last hour looking for you. I was just hoping to talk to you - I wanted to see how you're doing. I know you've been staying in a different spot..."

She looked at him sharply. "How do you know anything?"

Keith shrugged. "Well, I'm here, you're here, and now you're running away. I drove to the house in Bethesda after stopping by the office, you know. People are concerned, Jina. I told them Tony would be out for a bit, but they're asking questions. Look, this isn't about him so much - I just thought I'd check in. When you weren't in Bethesda and the place looked dead, I guess I thought you had been laying low with Robby somewhere else. Just wanted to see how you both were holding up and get an update on Tony? I know you're worried yourself," he finished pointedly.

"How he's doing? What? I don't know how he's doing. Hey, why are you here and not at the hospital if you're so concerned about how he's doing?"

"J, hey now - wait a minute. I just wanted to, you know, check in, talk to you before I went to see him," stuttered Keith. "Uh, I don't know - I mean, I don't want to be shocked at what he looks like... I just don't like hospitals. Do you know what's going on? - is he OK?"

"He's fine," she answered. "It wasn't as bad as they thought. His back is a little bit messed up, but he's going to recover. He just needs to go to rehab - he'll be fine, but thanks."

She completely omitted the part about the amnesia – well, if Keith was planning to see Tony then he could experience the shock of that part just as she had. It wouldn't hurt him nearly as bad as it did her.

"It's a good idea for you to go see him," she continued, warming to her subject. "Some familiar faces, will..." She trailed off: yet another lie. "You know, about Tony, uh, he probably won't know who you are," she tried again. "He doesn't...remember everything, and – well, I don't wanna talk about it. You know we're about to get a divorce. If you go see him, maybe you can help him: just be there for him."

And leave me be, she wanted to add. Keith and Tony were good friends and as far as she was concerned, they could just run off into the sunset together and leave her alone. She didn't care. Keith had always been all about money, all about Tony being at work all the time, watching and crunching the numbers for whatever they were supposed to be doing over at Tony's father's business. Tony had brought Keith on as a favor, and supposedly he'd risen to the task: a numbers genius, or at least that's what the business news outlets said. By all accounts, the company was turning around. Jina didn't quite know why she was so mean to him; but in her defense, he had always been too pushy: too involved and intertwined in their lives. Considering the whole divorce thing, it was hard not to resent his constant hanging around. She badly wanted distance from this man and Tony's stepmother, as well as anyone else lingering around their crumbling marriage.

"Well, amnesia? Say what? Ok – well, that's good to know," Keith replied in surprise. "I will make a trip over. Glad to hear he's doing all right physically at least."

"And another thing." She took a deep breath and stared at him coldly. "I've asked you before not to come over here anymore."

"Okay, Jina, but you know, I think - I thought, considering the issues, it would be all right this one time, huh?"

"Well it's not," she returned. "I meant what I said."

"Did you? You mean everything you say, Jina? I doubt it." Keith sighed. "You talk in contradictions. I hate to hear about you guys breaking up. You were just great together - meant for each other. I thought maybe, J, that... look, you're like my best friend too, all right? You... you know I've always had a fondness for you. I just thought that as his best friend, I, uh, should see how you're doing, you know. Is there anything I can do to help you and Robby? Maybe I could take him out to the park or something?"

Jina shook her head. She couldn't believe that Keith didn't have some ulterior motive. "No. Thank you," she added belatedly. "Robby is fine."

"Oh yeah? He's fine? Where is he?"

She hated that question. It was her fault, though: she didn't have to sit there and volunteer information. She should have said nothing at all.

"He's visiting with my sister," she said shortly, jabbing her key into the ignition as she put on her seatbelt. She was so done with all of this.

"Wow, uh, for how long, Jina? Tony's gonna want to see him, you know. It might speed his recovery."

That did it. "I'm sorry, are you questioning me?"

Keith raised an eyebrow. "I asked you a question, yes."

"Yeah, well, don't," she retorted. "It's none of your business. Listen, I don't owe you any explanations - I don't owe you anything. Just leave me alone and do not come here ever again."

"I'm just saying, what if Tony asks? He'll want to know where his son is."

"And I will tell him, okay? It's not some secret that only you know. He's fine and he's safe. He doesn't even remember that he has a son."

She knew that came out loud and she didn't regret it. She wanted her child more than anything right then. And that hurt her more than the divorce decree. What if they all forgot about her?

She turned to stare straight ahead, unseeing.

"I'm sorry, could you just respect my wishes and not come here? Considering all that's happened, I don't wanna associate with Tony's friends, work, personal or otherwise - and you fit both categories, right?"

She didn't like to seem so forceful, but she had already asked him not to come around. She had learned that some places in her life should be off limits from people like Keith. Work people. It was that very slippage that had had her focusing on work so much that she lost sight. That was why she was so easily able to see it happening in Tony, too. And he had respected her wishes, ensuring they only did business at the office or elsewhere outside home. Maybe that's where Tony had grown tired of her. She had no clue. That's how out of the blue his request for a divorce had been. It had come out of nowhere and punched her. It made her sick to her stomach, considering the secrets she kept.

This wasn't the first time Keith had disregarded her. The

more she looked at him, the more she resented his very presence. She wouldn't blame anyone for her and Tony's rift. She always wanted to be honest with herself, no matter what. But the longer she observed the people around her husband, the more she harbored resentment for every one of them. Still, the largest portion was aimed at herself.

Moreover, this house was sacred. She and Tony had never fought there. This house had seen three generations run through it and she wanted it to continue being her safe haven. That was all. She certainly didn't need him taking it upon himself to comfort her. Keith Munroe, despite his attempts, wasn't the man she wanted, ever.

"OK, OK, Jina." Keith raised both hands in mock surrender. "I'm sorry, I'll back off. I got it. I'll give you the space you need."

If anything, she wanted to ask him what Tony had told him the night of his car accident. She didn't have any facts - only a phone call telling her that he was severely hurt and that she should come to the hospital.

Jina adjusted her seat belt. When Keith straightened up, she rolled up the window. They were done with this conversation - and *done*, period, she dared hope. She revved the engine. As she pulled away, he stood there quite still on the sidewalk, hands in his pockets, just staring at her once again. She forced herself to look straight ahead. One day, she hoped, she could get all these people out of her mind - and her life - once and for all.

* * *

JINA COULDN'T SLEEP that night. No amount of counting sheep, warm milk or even reading a most uninteresting story could put her mind at rest. She wasn't used to sleeping alone, and since Robby was gone, even he couldn't be her companion.

She had been able to talk to Robby and Tish that night, though, as she did every night, which brought her a temporary relief and joy. She'd set a date with Tish and Chase to come get him. Though it was still a couple of days away, she was encouraged by the thought that she'd get her baby soon - but the past threats still made her a little crazy. Next on her list was to talk to an attorney about her custody rights.

Deciding it was finally time to confront the day, she put on her usual uniform of leggings and an oversized shirt and went to the kitchen for some ice water. Her tiny Alexandria apartment was still crammed with boxes that needed to be unpacked and put away. So far, she'd got out only what she needed and nothing more. She had set up Robby's tiny room, but that was only because she wanted him there so badly. Readying it for him gave her at least some purpose.

Though she was determined to move on with her life as a single person, she was still a mom, and that would make all the difference in the world to her. She missed him dearly, despite talking to him on FaceTime every night. She was glad Robby had Tish, as well as Alfreah, her own mother, and Tish's twins. They were younger than Robby, but it was still nice that he was getting to know his baby cousins. Just being around Tish and her happy family – Tisha's step-son Thomas, whom she treated as her own flesh and blood, Chase, and her mother - made Jina feel better about everything. Her mother had even offered to come and stay with her for a time. She knew her mother liked being there in Macon, and she knew the painful past that had caused her mother to leave in the first place. It made her brain hurt to revisit that twisted and crazy thing from last summer. Rather than make her mother feel guilty, then, she'd opted to leave Robby with them.

It was a decision she was regretting, especially with new thoughts about Tony, the pain that felt almost like abandonment, plus the new secret she'd discovered a week ago. She didn't know how long Tony's memory would be gone, but what if he did ask about their son? Would he understand why she did what she did?

Luckily, she didn't live far from her mother's home. Although her mother hadn't yet come back to Virginia, Jina had deliberately chosen to rent an apartment in Alexandria just in case. This way, Jina could be at her mother's in an instant. Had her mother been there, she might even have stayed with her and Robby. She could stay there now, in fact, considering her dwindling cash flow. With her impending divorce, she just wanted to get her bearings and some control over who turned up at her door.

Lately, however, all of her decisions felt poorly timed and probably didn't look like sound decisions at all. In fact, it was her way of taking control. She had to do something, she told herself - for herself and her sanity.

Her mother would return as soon as Tisha's twins turned two years old - *or she may not ever return*, the little voice reminded her. Regardless, she and Robby would be reunited... and she'd be a single parent, of him and the other tiny person developing inside of her. She'd make it work somehow. She wasn't giving up her son: not to anyone, not even his own father. Tony wasn't going to take him away from her, not without a fight.

Formerly a workaholic, Jina had never had time to for dinners and events. She'd worked so hard at her job and had moved up fairly swiftly, so when she got fired for protecting the very family that she shunned, she hit the bottom hard. She knew sometimes that's what it took, though: it was a wake-up call if ever there was one. Today, a new day, she knew where she stood with everyone and was determined to get herself back up and move forward.

Right about then, she knew an iced coffee would really help. She laughed: she'd swung from conquering her life issues to sugared-out snacks. Rome wasn't built in a day. Trying to be healthy, however, she settled for water. She turned on the faucet and washed her hands before opening the cupboard, grabbing her favorite tumbler and filling it with ice, then adding water. Maybe she'd do her blogging on the terrace today - it was really nice out. However, sandwiched as she was between an Indian couple on one side and a Korean-American family on the other, the rich and savory cooking smells were sometimes a little too pungent.

She made a mental note to add "learning to cook baby food recipes and small apartment living" to her blogging adventures. That was something that had started out as just some time for her, to fill the no-longer-a-journalist feeling. She still needed to create and write − plus, according to many therapists, it helped her work through her issues. She blogged under an assumed name, staying mostly down to earth but touching occasionally on the grief of loss, her miscarriages, her father's death a year ago, and a job she'd done for so long. While she had yet to touch the subject of divorce, she resolved that even if she did eventually experience it, she wasn't going to share about everything. She had over a million followers and received frequent letters from moms, even some dads. It gave her something to focus her energy on.

Remembering the potential food smells, she decided against her outside work place idea. She'd been especially sensitive to smells with this pregnancy. The bathroom was too far away in case of a nausea attack, so she often opted for water for the better part of her mornings until she felt pretty stable.

The tumbler pressed cold into her hand and she looked at it, noticing some scratches on one side: a souvenir of the fall she'd taken the day before that had garnered strange looks from Keith. He always seemed to look at her in a disapproving manner, a constant smirk on his face. She hated it. One deep mark featured a streak of darkened dried blood. She resisted the urge to scratch it. Annoyed with herself, she dismissed the scrape and proceeded to sip from her tumbler. The cold water and the ice to crunch would be welcome on such a hot day. She could finish her writing, conduct her online class and then – who knows? - she just might pack up to take her trip to Georgia and reclaim her son.

A new kind of panic suddenly stopped her in her tracks. What if Tony remembered and went down to get Robby before she did? She breathed hard, knowing she couldn't stand even the thought. Despite the intensity, though, she managed to stop herself from spiraling. She had learned some techniques to handle the fear that always threatened her. She sat on the bed and breathed. She told herself the stuff she needed to hear: the affirmations, the calming techniques a therapist had told her. The things that brought her off the ledge.

"I'm in control."

"No one will harm me."

"The people I love are safe."

Then the rational thinking:

"Tish would call me.

She wouldn't let Robby go without telling me.

She might even call the police.

He'd need a court order or something; they'd have to discuss it with an attorney.

It couldn't just happen."

As the doubts pounded in with each statement, she batted them away. It was hard - really hard – but she was doing it. She moved to the living room again, to reset, regroup.

She did it. Proud of herself: proud of not panicking to the extent that she'd needlessly bothered Tish and Chase with worry, or interrupted whatever fun family activity they were doing today.

A knock sounded on the door. She thought of a number of visitors it might be, but dismissed her friends, most of whom were working, and her family - also working or out of town. Curious, she put her phone in her back pocket and reached to open it.

The moment she saw who stood there, the panic rushed back. The air was sucked out of her lungs and the tumbler smashed to the floor, sending freezing cold water over her bare feet and toes. She couldn't feel a thing - she could only see Tony in front of her, standing tall and imposing at her door.

4

She lifted her feet, her hands reflexively grabbing to hitch up her pant legs, and navigated on tiptoe around the larger pieces of the broken tumbler to her carpeted living area. Sitting down to dry her feet, she watched in disbelief as Tony calmly walked in and shut the door behind him. She really didn't believe that he was there. At last, she found her voice.

"What are you doing here, Tony?

Without answering her, Tony set down a cup featuring the familiar logo of the green woman and mountains. He busied himself cleaning up the mess, wincing only slightly from the pain in his back. Jina watched in amazement.

"What do you mean, 'what am I doing here'?" he answered eventually, without looking up. "Don't I live here?" He winced again. "I hope to God I can get up."

He smiled at her, but she just stared back at him for what felt like an age, feeling as if she'd entered the twilight zone, before reaching out and offering him a hand up. He grinned and she flinched in annoyance.

"I'm all right," he reassured her. "I just probably shouldn't have done that." Putting a hand on his knee, he managed to haul himself up and leant against the counter momentarily, a hand on his back. "Just seeing if you were really a nice person, that's all," he chuckled.

Jina grew angrier.

"This isn't your house," she returned. "*I* live here. *You* live in our - your - Bethesda home. That's it."

"Well that was too far away from the hospital," he replied cheerfully. "I calculated the distance. Geez, with this traffic, I was glad I came here. Oh hey" – he handed her the cup – "this is for you. According to my route suggestions, I usually do this every other morning. They wrote your name on it, so I assume it's for you."

She took it in surprise. "Why on earth - what made you...?" She trailed off, amazed.

"It's morning, so according to the morning routine check-list I found on my phone and my buying history from the last few days, it's part of my usual routine to bring you this – oh, and normally a cake pop too, but they were out today. I didn't know what to bring instead so I didn't get anything, although I did remember that you liked butter croissants. I almost got that."

Jina smiled in spite of herself. She held the cup close and took a sip. *God is real,* she thought to herself as she tasted the caramel and vanilla crème drizzle. She actually needed to check the caffeine amount before she finished the entire thing in one gulp. Thankfully it was only the medium size. *Way to grow a baby that's as on edge and strung out as herself.* She took another sip for fortitude to deal with the man that now stood in her tiny kitchen, offering her things like nothing had ever transpired between them. She was confused.

A part of her wanted to cry. Despite not knowing her anymore, the fact that he'd actually researched his old routine was remarkable; and the fact that he was miraculously okay was blowing her mind. She had to admit she cared. It also meant he kept Siri's silly routine alarms on his phone, for her.

By contrast, she'd spent the day happily erasing the ones she had for him. Pick up dry cleaning, do an order for steak and potatoes and other food he liked, drive by the shops to collect the items. He did most of the cooking.

"What, uh, what… are you okay?"

"I'm all right, just couldn't take the blasted place any longer. Do you have a mop?"

She shook her head.

"Well, stay away from the door for a bit. I'll wipe this up, then when it dries I'll sweep or vacuum up the rest of the glass."

That statement sent alarm bells whirring in her brain. She remained silent as she watched Tony clean up the mess at her feet. She didn't know what to say. She remembered the doctor's advice about not giving him lots of information at one time. She wanted to tell him where his house was, draw him a map, do whatever she had to do to get him out of her place.

"So uh, what are you planning to do? Uh, did you need directions to the house?" she ventured.

"No, I'm not going there. I thought you and I could talk, see if some of my memory comes back?"

"Oh, oh, we're just gonna… chat?" She tried to keep the anxiety out of her voice but it didn't work. Her eyes were wide, she was sure: it was something she couldn't help.

"I thought you'd have a little mercy on me. I did just get out of the hospital."

"Oh – uh…" She wanted to be sympathetic, but that had dried up.

"I know, okay J? - Do I call you J?"

She nodded. That was one among numerous other familiar names she loved and hated equally - but she would tell him none of them.

He looked as if he mulled the letter over, assessing her.

"I can imagine I call you lots of little nicknames," he said thoughtfully. "You seem worthy of all of all them. All good, but many colorful ideas just seemed to pop into my head as you hesitated."

She shrugged, not giving him a clue one way or the other. His assessments, even right in line with her own thoughts, didn't mean she had to tell him that they were so spot on, not to mention that it gave her a little bit of hope. Whoever Tony King was before the divorce decree might still be in there, somewhere.

"Soooo," he continued and he smiled.

She hated it.

"You told me we were getting divorced, Jina," he continued. "I just - the only thing I really want to know right now is... why?"

She had a reason for her anger and it was on again. She looked up accusingly, slowly, and he leaned back only a little. She laughed falsely.

"Yeah, you know, that's a great question." She reached for her caffeinated sippy cup again.

"Shoes," he cautioned.

She rolled her eyes and did a quick about-face to grab some flip-flops. She snatched her cup from where he'd set it and, after a sip, realized she was going to need about two gallons of it. "Yes," she smacked her lips, more to the juju in the cup than to him. "But one problem."

"What?" He moved closer and she stepped back. His outstretched hand was akin to a surrender. She wasn't surrendering. She was going to have to stick to her guns at all costs.

No matter, she reasoned with herself: he'd brought her coffee, a really and truly thoughtful gift. Never mind that he'd almost died and left her without a husband and her child without a father. Whether together or apart, that pained her the most. That part she couldn't bear, and no matter the fact that he looked genuinely concerned and confused, she still hated it. Hated how it made her feel. "Well, Sherlock, sadly I already told you: I don't know the answer to your question."

5

There was only one thing that Tony King knew for sure: he was glad to be anywhere but in a hospital feeling alone and depressed. He didn't even know what he was depressed about. All he knew was that he'd felt relief when that first woman left; but then when the pretty one left as well, his depression had set in full throttle. Now that he was away from the hospital, he could work on getting back his sanity.

Only two days passed and the other woman came. Why on earth she kept visiting was beyond him. He didn't even know who she was. She also didn't listen to him when he told her to stop coming around. It grated on his nerves. She just scrutinized him a little too much, hoping for his memory to return. Not only that, she also asked a barrage of questions that only made his brain hurt.

By comparison, the younger woman – the one he could tell that he felt something for just by feeling his heart accelerate whenever she was around – seemed to want absolutely nothing to do with him.

He felt the little bad boy on his shoulder laughing at him. a deep, belly-shaking hoot. *Way to go! Ever since you were a kid,*

Tone, you still on the unlucky side, he thought to himself. As much as he had hoped for the last day and a half, this particular woman, Jina Jameson - his wife - hadn't returned at all.

If she wasn't coming to see him, he was dead set on going to her. It was she, he felt, who had the answers, and he needed them desperately. The other woman? Even her voice and her smelly perfume got on his nerves.

"Um, hey, sorry." He gestured to his attire, or what little there was of it. "Do I have any clothes here?"

"I need to eat, I mean - I mean – um," she said and moved to the kitchen. He followed her.

"Oh my God, don't follow me okay!" she exclaimed. "Sorry - yes, there's some sweats and a t-shirt on the top shelf in the closet."

"Toothbrush?" he questioned, trying to keep the hope from his voice. He wouldn't have asked if she'd said he didn't have clothes there, in her house, in their supposed state of divorce. Instead he might have taken the *no*, and asked if there was a washing machine and dryer where he could wash his clothes really quick, or a robe, or something, anything that could buy him some time to stay there with her, because he just had to stay. A part of him wanted her so bad: craved to experience whatever it was like between them in bed, then figure out the rest later.

"It's under the sink in your toiletry bag."

He didn't let her see his grin as he left her alone to search for the clothes. There was more to this story and he planned to get all the details, as many as she was willing to give, for as long as it took. Much to her dismay, probably.

In the back bedroom, Tony discarded the too tight short-shorts and mini shirt courtesy of the hospital's best offerings, throwing them in the trash. After a quick shower, he exited feeling refreshed and didn't bother with drying off: he'd air dry. He didn't put the fresh smelling undershirt on right away, but when he looked down, he saw a pair of man's slippers. He put his feet in them tentatively and, because he didn't feel a gross sensation and they seemed to fit, he assumed they were his. Shrugging his shoulders, he moved to the bathroom, opening the under-sink doors. Not only was there a toothbrush, there was also a leather travel case. It took sheer force of will not to smile. Surely there were people who tried to divorce and for whatever reason didn't: maybe the process was too long, or they had a few more flings before they actually called it off, perhaps because they were each still needy and needing. He hoped for the latter, and that this was the case here too, because they were still in love. Ain't that something?

The more he thought about the facts, the more his mind tried to create logical order: make sense of it, build timelines, maybe even play a little devil's advocate with asking the tougher questions, in spite of the small things that gave him glimpses of hope. Everything, however, was coming so fast that his brain hurt.

He had stuff there: okay, thumbs up, great. But only a few things. Plus, the closet was pretty bare. Then again, the place was also bare of her own stuff, and boxes littered the living room. She wasn't long into the place and she hadn't unpacked, or maybe she hoped to come back - yes, she hoped to come back and they'd reconcile, and...

He felt defeated again. Amidst all her shirts, jeans and slacks, he might have seen only one other thing that looked like it was a man's size. He left his toiletry bag there on the counter and studied himself in the mirror. He looked at the bag again, noticing the piece of soft leather on the zipper pull embossed with his own initials. He touched the soft leather and traced the ridges of his name. Thoughtful gift. *You're the king of the castle, my man,* he assured himself, even as more doubt battled against the little hope he had managed. He stared back at himself in the mirror as he rolled on the brand of deodorant he apparently wore, then donned the crisp white t-shirt before refilling the bag, closing it so hard the little pull ripped a little.

He stopped and stilled, hearing a metallic sound. He opened the bag wide and saw something in the bottom of it: a shiny object that glinted in the light. It rolled away as he tried to grab it amongst all the other contents. When he finally pulled it out, he quickly looked at both his hands, realizing they showed not one sign that he was married. Before putting it on, he inspected the wedding band closer, In perfect condition as far as he could tell, a tiny inscription in a fancy black script nestled inside its curve. He squinted to make it out: *Our love. Undeniable.*

It was like sign, a kick in the gut. He took a deep breath as thoughts came over him once again, like a wave. He wasn't giving up. Dismissive of the vague digging guilt, he slipped the ring onto the appropriate finger and flexed his hand. It fit. Perfectly. It was his. If he had removed it before, he sure as hell wasn't going to remove it a second time. Someone must have wrestled him to get it off.

He stared again. Surely he had taken it off for some reason. Why would he do that? Surely she didn't take it off him? And if she had been able to, why put it in the bag here, mixed up with mostly her stuff? And why did he have stuff here at all? Because it wasn't over: he'd evidently been there with her, in some capacity or another, within the last month. Perhaps reconciling? He could only hope, and that was the thought he would hold onto, at least until he had a better reason and a solid handle on what happened. He wasn't ready to let go. He couldn't, not yet.

Shaking his head in bewilderment, Tony replaced the items into the bag and replaced the bag itself under the sink. His stuff was there for a reason. He turned off the light, closed the door, and almost stomped in the comfy slippers back to the front.

He slowed as he heard voices. Jina was talking with someone, a male this time. He didn't recall having heard a doorbell or the sound of someone coming in.

When he came into the kitchen this time, there was another man talking to Jina, and she did not look happy about it. Never having wanted to believe anything about the divorce, now that he saw her with another man, he wondered if this could be the person that had come between them? Perhaps it wasn't about him at all, but about her relationship with someone else. It angered him like nothing else he'd ever felt in his life.

* * *

"HERE'S TONY - EXCUSE ME."

"Wait, Jina, we're not..."

"No, no. You two talk," she insisted.

Tony saw her eyes turn somewhat kind to him before she eased her arm away from his touch. "We can finish when you guys are done. *He* has been wanting to talk to you." She cast angry eyes back at the stranger.

Tony watched Jina leave, but as he turned and found the man's gaze lingering on her back, he scrutinized him a little more closely. His focus seemed to sharpen with the slam of the door behind her.

"The doctors said you were a miracle man, but my goodness. Check you out."

The man before him grinned and moved closer. Tony hadn't initiated the contact and he felt odd: was he a hugger? He didn't feel like one, especially not now. To thwart the contact, he stuck his hand out, even as the man moved into his personal space. They did the awkward hug, - the hug from bro types, he supposed - with a pat on the back and a side handshake. Tony stepped back. He was tall, but the man before him was very muscular. Tony took in the bulging biceps beneath the tight-fitting tailored suit.

"Bruh, how are you, for real? Oh hey man, oh my God. You're a freaking miracle." Tony just smiled tightly and nodded.

"That's what they say," he replied. "Doctors say I still need some rehab but I'm feeling good." He tried to smile, tried to make contact but otherwise he couldn't get onboard with the warm-and-fuzziness. If the man before him was a friend, why hadn't he come to the hospital?

"Yeah, you in real good shape, you old slugger, for real - but uh, Jina, she told me you had amnesia. Listen, man, I'm Keith, by the way. Keith Munroe. I'm actually your business partner. We work at your dad's outfit together."

"Really?"

"Yeah, really. Everyone at the office is going to be so happy you're okay. It's amazing. You feeling okay?"

"A little tired, meds are wearing off, but I'm good."

Tony wanted to talk to Jina alone, but now they'd moved beyond the kitchen to the living room and there was no sign of her. He wondered what she was doing. Would she give him any new information when he got done talking to this guy? Tony continued to scrutinize him, trying to recall just what kind of friends they were. Truth be told, the man grinned too much and used to much slang. Tony was tired. He kind of remembered him, and the fact that they might have been friends.

"How long have we known each other again?" he enquired.

"Aw man, we go way back. I introduced you to Jina."

"Really?"

"Yeah. Say, you talk like you don't believe me. We were really cool back in the day."

Tony shrugged. Should he believe him? He didn't believe anyone; he had no idea what to think, really. "And we - the both of us - work for my father?" Tony clarified.

"Well, you know, you wanted to make it work while your

father was getting old and sickly, so you know, I thought it was a good opportunity. Then you hired me. The two of us have been real good for the business. You're really turning things around - with my help, of course."

Tony frowned. He'd never quite forgiven his father for leaving him as a child and beating up on his mother. The idea that he was not only working for his old man now but that things were actually going well seemed more ludicrous than all the other crazy ideas floating around his brain. The more he listened, the more it seemed completely unreal.

"Listen, you know, you go ahead and take a few days off. You gotta go to rehab or what?" asked Keith.

"They mentioned it," Tony said evasively. The truth was, he had rushed from the hospital and had zero intentions of returning. If he had to go to rehab, he hoped it was in a different building, off-site. He should find a brain specialist that could somehow hypnotize his memory back, because right then that was a priority right up there with figuring out his marriage situation. The doctor had given him the all-clear to leave but told him he shouldn't drive - and though he'd desperately wanted to, he'd asked for help to figure out the ride share app to get him to his destination. The jostling hurt a little with the crazy driver's stop start jerking approach to driving, but he'd otherwise arrived safely. The second piece of advice was to watch for blinding headaches, as his brain worked to untangle the wiring. He had a couple of prescriptions, but he'd tossed those in the bathroom trash. He was fine, he was sure, except for the fatigue.

"Say, do the authorities have any ideas on how your car crashed?"

Tony looked up. The question added another layer of things he needed to know more about. He had assumed it was an accident. A wet road, a steep hill, a curve - and what? He had no idea.

"No, no word," he answered slowly. "They are still investigating it. Why do you ask?"

"No reason. Hey, I just don't want nothing happening to my friend, you know?"

Tony nodded but didn't return Keith's grin.

"Well, look, I know how stubborn you are, so please just don't neglect that rehabilitation stint, okay? You gotta be good, you gotta be one hundred percent. Can't have the top executive ill and out of commission - not when we're about to turn this company around and announce new leadership, okay?"

"What leadership?" Tony asked, nonplussed.

"Oh man, all right, I'll tell ya: you're going to be company President, okay?" Keith beamed at him: a wide, toothy smile. "There's a board meeting next month and, well, you're up. Your father wants you to take the reins. We just have some more things we need to do get it all in order."

"Are you serious?" Tony did a double take. His jaw twitched. He'd not only decided to work for his father but to take control of the company, too? This just didn't sound right. He took a deep, weary breath.

"Tony, you're a good dude."

Tony scrutinized the man in front of him and tried not to shrug off the hand Keith placed on his shoulder. As much as the statement made him feel better, the evidence wasn't in agreement. It confused him.

"Trust me on this. You know, you grow up, you forgive, you move on. Come on man, it happens. I say he's trying to make amends before he kicks the bucket, you know?"

"He's getting sick, he's dying - what happened?" Tony didn't know how he felt. This was a lot of information. If he was about to own a company, he'd forgiven his father, and said company was turning around, then why was his marriage in the can - and all in a matter of eighteen months, too? He felt like he had whiplash from the thoughts alone.

"Yeah, something like that," Keith answered casually. "He has this cancer thing, they said. But look, ask Jina about it. And listen, I really want to talk to you but uh, it's better if we talk business at your other spot, you know?" Keith leaned in, his voice barely above a whisper. "Your old lady doesn't take too kindly to business talk. She don't like it, you know?"

"Why is that?" Tony questioned.

"Ah, you know how these – ah, females are. And that new stepmommy you got, she ain't real keen – well, they ain't real keen on each other. Wait till you meet her."

"I already met her."

"Oh, well then, I hope she and Jina ain't..." Keith mimed a boxing move, an upper cut and a jab. Tony instinctively put his hands up, slapping the hand away.

"There's the man, you still got stuff up there," Keith laughed, tapping his own temple. "So, you know there'll be a knock-out fight between those two if you leave 'em for too long, okay. And you know I love a good fight, so the thought of those two going at it..." Keith laughed. "I don't know, it'd be something to see. I'd pay the big bucks, for real." Keith grinned again.

"You like that, women fighting, seriously?" Tony asked incredulously. Even if Keith was joking, the image he conjured was horrible, not to mention the protective feeling that came over Tony thinking about Jina in that situation. Who on earth joked about stuff like that? He disliked this man more and more by the minute. He was rude, he took nothing seriously and he joked too much.

"Hey man, yeah women fighting, you know, put 'em in something skimpy, add a little mud, watch 'em duke it out." Keith's smile broadened. "Aw, you know I'm just playing man. Jina would beat yo' step-momma to the ground. Your wife is certifiable." Keith chuckled and the sound grated on Tony's nerves. "But for real, don't ya go making your ex mad okay?" Keith lifted a finger and twirled it against his temple. "So, I just wanted to check on you, see how you doing. I'ma go. Jina thinks I'm always bothering you. I went to the hospital and you had already checked out and... well, she don't like me coming to the house to talk shop and all. Let me know when you get back to Bethesda. I'll come over there, then we can talk some more."

Tony was elated he was leaving. "Thanks for coming." he said as he moved to the door. "I think I'm taking it easy for a week or so. I don't plan to go there any time soon."

Truly, if Jina wasn't there, he wanted no part of that Bethesda place. There was a pic of it on his phone. While it loomed large, all lit up in the photo, his phone also held messages he hadn't yet had time to explore between him and what appeared to be a realtor, asking him about a timeline for its sale. Another contradiction, another mystery. If he was giving up his house and they were getting a divorce, where on earth did he have plans to move to – and why?

"All right, all right. Hey, uh, are y'all getting back together?" Keith ventured. "Hey, sorry, don't answer if you're uncomfortable, but I'ma wish you luck on that. I guess if anyone can convince her, it's a former lover."

Keith said his goodbyes and Tony shut the door with finality and locked it. When he turned back, Jina was standing in the kitchen, her arms crossed over her chest and her large eyes indicating a storm on the horizon.

* * *

JINA GLARED AT HIM, even as she could hardly get the image of his torso from earlier out of her mind. The entire time he'd been in there talking to his bro, she was in the back starving to death while also going stark raving mad. The last thing she had wanted was for Keith Munroe to show up at her house. Even if Keith had called ahead, she considered, Tony may well have conveniently ignored the message as he usually tended to: with or without functioning memory, she recollected, he never answered texts. Thus, Keith just kept popping up seemingly unannounced - even when she'd specifically asked just the day before that he leave her alone. She usually felt safe here; now she was discombobulated all over again, just as she had been when she'd awoken from the impromptu nap on her porch to find him cradling her a little too intimately. She felt on edge again. Her nerves were just a mess.

"Could we talk a little?" Tony ventured.

Jina shook her head and moved around him. Resolute, she reached for a long stick that she kept on the floor by the door. She pushed the security bar under the door's knob and used her foot to wedge it tightly in place. She tapped in a number and the sounding beat went off, indicating that the outside alarm was set for the night.

"Are you scared?" he asked.

"No I'm not scared. I just don't want any more unexpected visitors," she replied.

"Are you sure? Are you scared of me?"

"Of course I'm not scared of you, Tony. I just locked you in here with me – well, sorta. Would I do that if I were scared of you?"

"Just making sure, okay? Why are you so angry and on edge?"

"I'm annoyed and... hungry," she said, softening a little. "Hey, in the future, please ask your little friend Mr. Munrow to call you first, and make an appointment to meet him somewhere other than my house. I don't like him."

"Join the club," Tony said, rolling his eyes.

With the door secure, Jina looked back at Tony with a confused face, surprised by his statement. "He's your best friend - how can you not like him?" she asked, bewildered.

"Well, you don't like him, and I'm on Team Jina; plus, something about him rubs me the wrong way," he answered. "And for you to put a security bar at the door, I figure he must have done or at least said something pretty extreme. Or is there, like, a serial killer around or something?"

"How do you know you don't like him? You don't even remember stuff - and you being on Team Jina? Thanks and all, but that's a complete lie."

She didn't want to pick a fight with him, but it seemed like it might be the only way to send him packing. He could not stay another minute, despite what the availability of clothes, toothbrush and house slippers might indicate about their situation.

"First, I want to say that I'm sorry for whatever I did to you, Jina."

"Don't - please, don't. I can't take it and I'm not going there."

"I want you to tell me Jina," he continued. "It's killing me to know that I did something, that we are broken, that everything is so confusing. That I forgave my father - why the hell would I do that? Why am I working for him? And what kind of partner is Keith Munroe, anyway? He's a fast-talking, money-grubbing know-nothing. My father... oh my God, my father, and Keith!" he repeated incredulously. "He and I really work for my father. And who cares about all that anyway, Jina? The main question is, why are we not together? And why does this wicked stepmother keep brothering me? I have a second chance and I can't blow it now."

She didn't want to look up at him, but she did.

"God gave me a second chance. I'm a miracle. I walked away from a crashed and burned out car – now I have to figure out some crap. *This* is crap. I have a second chance to make this right, to fix something. I cannot do it without you. Aren't you glad I'm okay, Jina?"

"So now you're giving me a guilt trip?"

"I'm not," he defended. "Hey, let me make you something to eat. You tell me stuff, I'll cook. I feel like that works. Okay?"

She watched him hurry to the kitchen. She didn't want to,

but hunger seem to weaken her resolve not to blurt out the one secret she held – two, if she counted Robby. At that moment, she was just drained. The day felt long already and it was barely lunchtime. Her morning sensation of peace had fizzled out. She remained calm, only she knew she was about to break.

At the sink, he washed his hands and dried them with paper towels. When he went to the fridge, he looked at her, raising his eyebrows. "How about an omelet?"

Her hope grew and she tried not to smile, though she knew it was too late. He saw her grin, try as she might to hold onto her anger. She could be bought with food.

"Oh I got it, I'm onto something, huh? I'd say that's about all you got in here anyway. Let's see: bacon, cheese, onions... well, someone's priorities are in order..."

Jina took a seat at the table. She wasn't even sure how to *be* almost-divorced. She took a deep breath. Despite not wanting to admit that she'd needed more than the measly turkey sandwich she was going to make, Tony knew she couldn't turn down his cooking. He could cook, she could eat; it all comes out in the wash, she thought to herself.

"Tony, uh, we're getting a divorce. You, uh, you have a house in Bethesda and..."

She trailed off, distracted watching his hands work. The way he cut the veggies to sauté them before throwing them into the eggs. His hands were nice, his fingers long... She looked away.

"Sounds far, where is that?" he asked.

"What?"

"Bethesda?"

Jina frowned. *Focus, girl. Hormones are raging at your baby daddy, but come on. He's not really that nice. He's confused about everything. He's confusing you, for that matter.* She hadn't been eating right, though, so she was in no position to turn him down - not that her stomach would let her.

"You like my cooking, don't you? I think that's how I won your heart, no?"

"Can we not?"

"Okay, but back to the omelet. Where's the salt and pepper? Oh, and you were saying? Where's Bethesda?"

"Look, I'm just gonna be straight up here, Tony."

"Seems that's how we are to each other usually, isn't it?" he questioned. She smiled and he liked that. He loved her.

"We really shouldn't prolong this. You'll get your memory back and we'll be back to where we were."

"To, getting a divorce?"

"Yes, that's where we were." *And where we are*, she thought bitterly. She hated to admit it, but to have the truth out meant she could protect herself better. None of the surprise of that unexpected notice, served to her by some mail worker. No signature on a digital pad as her heart broke right in front of the FedEx guy.

"Your eyes are beautiful, Jina. Look, if I caused this I want to know," Tony said. "Surely you have some inkling about why I did it."

His hand reached out to caress her face but, though she would have relished his touch at any other time, now she turned her face away. She steeled herself against him: against any attempt to reach through the wall she was still building back up around her heart. It was weak; it probably wouldn't be able to withstand him until more time had passed. She counted to ten: she had to be strong.

"Bethesda isn't far, it's uh, just about 30 minutes."

"Doctor says I shouldn't drive for a few days."

"Um, she closed her mouth thinking.

"I took a ride share," he defended reading her mind. "It was ten miles, and I was highly motivated, I had to get here to see you. I missed you."

She laughed, only it wasn't anything genuine, it was bitter and hollow. It hurt. "You got me a coffee." She said more to herself not realizing it came out. She was still in awe over that.

"Because I care about you, and the reminder came in my phone, oh and the Starbucks is in the building, not to mention it's obviously something I do on the regular."

Jina blew out a breath: she'd put the reminder on his phone herself. "Tony, just..." She let it go. She kept her eyes on him, on his back, on the way the thin t-shirt fitted him, outlining his muscles as he moved. Now and then, when his eyes lingered on hers, she resisted the urge to touch her cheek, recalling his caress. He turned and she started to avert her eyes, annoyed, but then glanced back at him with renewed curiosity. How in the world it was possible that he stood there before her amazed her. She did thank God he was okay: she was in love with him – so it hurt all the more.

He opened the door to the fridge to retrieve the eggs. The vegetables sautéing in the pan sent good smells around the small place, and her mouth watered. She closed her eyes, savoring the moment.

Suddenly she heard a gasp. Two eggs crashed to the floor as she saw Tony stagger to the stove.

"Are you hurt?" she asked in alarm. "What's the matter? Tony - *Tony?*" Her heart felt like it would leap out of her chest. "What is it? What is it?" Her hands shook as they reached out to him.

It was almost as if he was fainting. He gripped the counter to steady himself as she snatched the block of cheese from his grasp, his muscled, sinewy form looming unsteadily over her. He saw her but didn't, she could tell: his mind was in some sort of fog. He put a hand to his head as if he was having a seizure, but his eyes focused and blinked, his breath coming in short bursts - she felt each breath through her fingers. He backed up to the wall behind him, leaning heavily against it, his eyes tightening as if in pain. Not sure what to do, she just held him, her hands around his stomach, the muscles rippling under her fingers as she just tried to be present to him. She'd carry him somehow, if she had to…

"What is it, talk to me, please, Tony?" she pleaded.

"Robby," he breathed out at last, on a ragged whoosh of air. His eyes met hers, searching desperately for answers.

She burst into tears, doubtless putting fear into his heart, because she felt like she really was in the wrong. She felt the guilt, the magnitude of everything finally taking its toll on her. It was all her fault their son wasn't there - but it was his fault too. He'd left her and it had hurt so bad. He forced her to abandon everything.

She looked up, drawing breath to speak, but he spoke first, his tone accusatory.

"We lost some of our children, Jina. Where's Robby - where's my son?"

6

"No, no!" Jina replied in alarm, wiping hastily at her eyes. "I mean, we lost children. Yes, I had some miscarriages - but not Robby. Robby is fine, Tony, he is safe. He's with my sister. He's in Macon, and he's fine - he is fine."

The tears came again – she couldn't stop them. Jina felt horrible that her son was not with them. Maybe having Robby with them in the flesh would have jogged Tony's memory about other things, too. She couldn't explain where Robby was right now – not satisfactorily, anyway. No amount of reasoning would justify it: her reasons for having given her child to her sister paled now, seeming to mean nothing. Now, it simply looked as though she had given up on everything and everyone.

Yes: it was all happening now. Before much longer Tony would remember why they were divorcing, and the fact that his son was not there with her would only count against her. Past bad decisions added fuel to the fire that was already burning out of control.

"We can call him," she said hurriedly, glad Tony was at least still standing. He seemed to have his footing back, though she noticed that he still touched his head periodically. Maybe it physically hurt, some result of the accident; or maybe it was just painful to remember all their losses. She gingerly moved away to get her phone, relieved that he hadn't succumbed to whatever it was that had suddenly hijacked his brain just then. He had looked like he was going into some kind of epileptic seizure. At least he hadn't ended up down on the tile floor with the broken eggs. She could not take any of that right now. As strong as she made herself out to be, in the last few weeks she'd felt like she was completely incompetent.

"I'll just... we can call my sister. Here I can FaceTime her."

Silently, Tony began cleaning up the mess of eggs - she noticed that he held the wall now as he bent down. She tried to focus, to ignore the cute picture of Robby and Tony beaming from her phone's wallpaper. It had been just the two of them: Tony looking ahead at the camera while Robby had eyes for only his daddy, trying to shove his little grubby fingers into his mouth. Her fingers trembled. She grabbed a tissue and wiped her eyes roughly, thankful that she had opted not to wear make-up. The last thing she needed was for her sister to think something was wrong, or that something had happened to her. What if she thought the worst and didn't let her come to get Robby? Suddenly she was desperate to get her entire family back under the same roof, as broken and as uncertain as it was. She felt panicked.

"It's okay, it's okay - whatever it is, I forgive you," came Tony's reassuring voice. "It's a good idea. We have a mess here. If you sent him because this was just too much, I understand."

She wanted to cry all over again. For a moment, he sounded like the Tony she knew long ago, kind and genuine. The one that loved her unconditionally and understood her. His strange episode seemed to be subsiding now. He was talking and seeming fine as she continued to try to pull up the stupid number and the right contact. Why did everyone have so many numbers?

Finally, the familiar Facetime bleeps got going. She waited, practicing normal-looking smiles into the phone camera, until eventually her sister came on the line. Tish's beautiful face staring back at her always knew what Jina wanted to see. Tish told her every day that she could and absolutely should come and get her child any time she wanted, day or night. That she would be there for her, but that she'd also give her the distance, time and space that she needed.

"Are you okay, sweetie? Jina? You okay?" came her sister's concerned voice.

Jina nodded, her voice catching: "Fine, fine." She cleared her throat, feeling like she was going to throw up. "I'm okay," she croaked weakly.

They talked every night. She saw Robby just like this every night, only it was earlier than her usual pre-bath time chat. Robby was always already in her sister's arms anticipating the call; if she didn't call, Tish called her.

"There's your Mommy! Robby, look!" Tish said. "Hey, Mommy. Mommy is doing great. Right, Robby?"

"Yes, yes, hey baby," Jina replied, the crack in her voice disguised by the gift of constantly-buffering technology. "Yes, yes, I'm fine. Hey, look who's here!" she said, trying to sound cheery. She turned the phone to include Tony in the screen's small display shot. Tony put his arm around her shoulder to get closer in, bending down, even bringing his breath closer to her ear.

She continued to coo at Robby until Tony took the phone and stood up to speak to his son, freeing her from his embrace. She moved away but continued to listen intently as Tish asked him about the accident and how he was doing. They made small talk, even as Robby was doubtless trying to get the phone out of Tish's hands, more interested in playing with it than in chatting. Jina moved to the other end of the apartment, where she could breathe. She could hear Tony talking to Robby, could hear Tish's numerous questions: not only about the two of them, but also about how Jina herself was doing.

Trying to get away, she went into the bathroom and shut the door. Closing the lid, she sat on the commode, her hands over her ears. She wanted to get Robby. She shouldn't have left him. She loved him so much, but she was getting divorced; she lost her job; she lost her whole life and, as much as she hated it, had been just unable to focus on her second, yet-unborn baby. Deep down, she was afraid she'd lose him or her too. Her hands rubbed her barely-there bump, wondering how long she could keep the secret - and what on earth was going to become of her, or her marriage.

She was about to get up when the door was wrenched open. She stared dumbly at Tony. He handed her the phone: there were nothing but her apps staring back at her, not Tish and certainly not Robby.

"I want my son," Tony intoned with certainty. "Tish said we can come anytime, so let's go get him, together."

"Okay," she returned and stood as if she was in the United States Marine Corps and had just been given a direct order. Even as she moved to the closet to pack an overnight bag, she wondered what earth she'd been thinking when she made that arrangement, as the agreement came so easily from her mouth.

* * *

SHE DIDN'T REALIZE he'd removed his loafers until she saw them turned over by the door. The spot where the eggs had been glistened fresh and clean; a whiff of disinfectant met her nostrils, making her feel just a tad nauseous.

Despite all but announcing their imminent departure for Macon, Georgia, she was surprised to find Tony calmly cleaning things and apparently preparing a second attempt at the omelet. Tossing the now burnt onions and mushrooms into the sink, he cleaned the pan to start the process all over again. He set the eggs in a bowl this time, and, after taking a deep, calming breath, beat them vigorously. She watched again and took a seat as he made the food, wordless for the longest time.

"I didn't mean to sound so urgent," he said at last. "We can go in a few days. I imagine the air pressure in the cabin of a plane will be the death of me right about now. So, uh, I'll just give it a few days. But, can I just..." He took a deep breath. "Why did you give him to her?"

"First of all" - she tried to ease her tone - "I did not give him up: I asked her to watch him for a few days. I wanted him to be happy and safe while I moved."

"When did you move?"

"Just over a week ago."

"When were you planning to go get him?"

"This week, until the accident. I was going through a lot and... well, if I had bad news to share, it was best that she kept Robby a few more days. I wanted to just see if you..." The unthinkable, she thought to herself.

"What, died?"

"No, I knew you hadn't died," she said impatiently. "They called me, plus it was all over the news. I just needed some time to figure out the divorce. I wanted Robby to be around happiness, and with his cousins. It was only supposed to be for a week, while I squared away some things, moved in here. It's not easy moving into an apartment with a toddler - you do understand that, don't you?"

"Why did you leave?" he replied.

Jina threw up her hands in exasperation. "Are you kidding? I'm sick of having this conversation. You wanna know so much? Well, out of the blue you came to our Bethesda home just weeks ago and you said you wanted out.

Out of nowhere, you said you wanted out. So, after much thought, I decided I didn't want that stupid too-big house anyway. I wouldn't be able to afford it after I got fired from my job. *You* sent the divorce papers – you! You wonder why your step-mom and Keith Munroe and whoever else keep showing up unwelcome and uninvited to get to you? Because you traded them for me!" She was yelling now. "You want money and status and toys, and all the power your daddy had in his prime, to resurrect a company that's not any good? And you and your friend take it over and take over the world. Is that how it's supposed to go? Good for you. So, in all that, somewhere you turned - you changed. And they very well may have killed you, in the form of that stupid self-driving car your dad bought you off with, not even on the market yet. Your need to get the latest and greatest almost cost me a husband, cost my child a father, and almost cost you your entire life - but that ain't nothing, I suppose. You were just ready to give it up. Before I could even get into this place, before I could even have the stupid mail forwarded, the first thing I got was a big old divorce decree. So excuse me while I don't give a care. I don't care. We're done."

"The house is going up for sale."

Jina was startled. "Why, where are you supposed to live?"

"I'm gonna live here, right here. I'm sorry for what I said, what I did, but I'm not getting a divorce. Where are those papers?"

"Why does it even matter?" she countered.

She watched as Tony set about hunting through every nook and cranny of the room in search of the papers. He rifled through the recipe books, notebooks and papers, before he finally noticed the stack of papers on top of the microwave, under a paperweight. Triumphantly, he pulled an official-looking document from the pile. It wasn't opened - she hadn't had the heart to open it. Maybe he'd ask her to sign it there and then. Maybe she would, just to be done, as much as it would pain her…

To her surprise, he suddenly held the envelope close to the gas stovetop ring, under the sauté pan. The flames immediately licked and lit the paper. He flicked it deftly into the sink and watched it burn to ashes, before rinsing them away.

"Looks like we're not getting a divorce. That's not what I want, ever. See this?" He pointed to his wedding band, his hand blurring in front of her face.

He expertly put the omelet on the plate, folding it perfectly to tuck in all the veggies, the bacon and the cheese peeking out of the edges. He got a fork and a napkin, plus the tiny bottle of hot sauce from her lazy Susan, and placed them by her plate. "Don't use too much, you'll get heartburn," he advised.

Jina smiled, amazed.

"Is your - is your memory back?" She was hopeful and scared at the same time.

"No, but I don't need it to remember that I have loved you for a very long time. So, I gotta lot of work to do convincing you that whatever the hell I did was a huge mistake. I am not – I mean, we are not over. Whatever I need to do next, short of some kind of brain transplant, I will do: hypno-therapy or what, I don't know. Just… you should know that no options are off the table, however drastic. I am going to figure this out."

He leaned in front of her and she instinctively moved back. His hand caressed the side of her face again, and gently grabbed her chin. Although she tried to turn her face, he managed to steal a kiss before standing up again.

She ate her omelet in silence as she waited for whatever crazy, mind-scrambling thing was going to happen to her next.

7

Two days passed quickly but awkwardly, and before long they were standing on the front stoop of her sister's gloriously beautiful house. Surprisingly at her insistence, Tony had called his doctor to get the medical verdict about driving versus flying, and accordingly they had found themselves driving the many hours to Macon, Georgia. She managed almost four hours driving straight from Alexandria and Tony managed the other half of the trip. Despite fighting sleep to keep an eye on him, she couldn't fight her fatigue for long, and when she woke up they were already there. As they approached, the bright lights along the front of the porch flipped on and before either of them could knock, the door opened to reveal Tish.

Jina took her sister in her arms, trying not to let her relief at seeing her for the first in almost a year get the best of her. Tish rushed forward, kissing her on the cheek and giving her the warmest hug. She pulled Tony in for an embrace too, and his arm came all the way around to Jina. She stiffened at how near his large right hand was to her belly. She broke away from their group hug, before smiling tightly through her tears.

"You look good," Tisha smiled. "Tony, I am so glad you're okay."

Tony nodded. "Thanks - me too!"

Tisha laughed and, looping arms with Jina, pulled her inside ahead of him. Chase appeared, taking their luggage and making greetings before seeing about fresh coffee, the aroma of which already filled the house. Tish led them to the living room where they all sat down.

Tish was still grinning at the sight of seeing her, but Jina knew the questions might soon ensue. She just wanted to get her child and go, as rude as that might seem: she wanted less talking and just to be back in Virginia by morning - but she and Tony had talked about staying at least for a night, so as not to just completely alter Robby's daily routine, whatever that was nowadays.

"I uh, Robby is doing good," Tish began. "He is probably up, so if you want to just go, I understand."

Tony sat on the edge of his seat but didn't make a move. Jina hesitated.

"Do – do you think he will, uh, miss it here, if we take him too quickly? Does he have any new things, toys, foods...?"

"You talk to him every day so you are up on everything," Tish laughed. "Anyway, he's only been here for three weeks, and he's seen you every single day online. He will be fine."

Jina nodded, looking away. "Three weeks seemed liked years."

"And whose fault is that?"

As Jina looked up abruptly, anger surging, she told her easily-hurt feelings to consider the source of the hurtful comments. It was sister: she didn't mean it like that. Jina knew as much, but it was hard not to bristle - especially when it was the truth.

"I'm sorry honey," Tish murmured.

"It's okay. I know you didn't mean it that way. I know," she assured her sister, seeing her look of sadness.

Chase returned with coffee. Though Jina had no intention of drinking it, she didn't want anyone to be suspicious of her refusal. At least it gave her something else to focus on, something to do with her hands to calm her nerves. She stared unseeingly down into the dark liquid. Chase handed the other to Tony, who took a hot sip and eased back into the sofa.

"So what are you up to? Are you in physical therapy, Tony, for your injuries?" Chase asked.

"Uh no, but I guess I should be. I've mainly been having memory issues. I also had this really bad headache the other day when I recalled something."

Tish and Chase nodded. Jina averted her eyes when she saw Chase place his hand on Tish's crossed legs. Tony looked over at her and she obviously gave him a look that could kill, so he looked straight ahead again. The gesture was not lost on either of them. Even in happier times, when things were perfect between she and Tony, they hadn't ever been the public, touchy-feely type of couple – or rather, she wasn't. It wasn't because she didn't want to be, or that she didn't love him - it was the past trauma that kept her keeping her hands to herself. She'd never gotten over it… but, she considered sadly, he'd probably forgotten all of that. Considering their current status, they certainly weren't in a position to start it now. There were ways to reach her, but he may never remember them, and that saddened her more than anything. Jina felt antsy. Unable to escape scrutinizing every thought she had, the majority of them negative, she couldn't make small talk any longer. She stood abruptly.

"Excuse me, I gotta… go to the rest room." She made an apologetic face and set her brim-full coffee cup down on a nearby table before exiting the room.

She really did have to go, but she also had an ulterior motive: to see Robby alone first. She quickly checked her face and wiped it with just a little cool water before exiting. The flush of her anxious desire to have any kind of touch or acknowledgement and a glimpse of the old Tony was going to grate on her nerves. Longing was not new to her, but it was something she wasn't sure she could handle at the moment. The last two nights had been torture: he slept in the guest room, which was also Robby's room, on a small day bed, and knowing he was not even ten feet away drove her crazy. Yes, they'd been together, yes she had proof of their intimacy, but the memory of it could never replace the real thing. He insisted on staying there with her, but if it was going to be, they could not, would not, share a bed.

Sexual frustration was something she'd never experienced before. She'd always had what she wanted. Now that things were different, it would take time and a whole lot of prayer to deny him what they had shared less than one month ago. Part of her wondered if his memory could be triggered back by some really good...

"Momma!"

"Hey baby."

Her awful thoughts scattered like roaches as her mother smiled. It took Jina's sheer force of will not to cry as the aging woman ambled toward her.

"How are you, baby?"

Jina sighed. Not only was she saddened about the sad shape of her life, she hadn't yet called on the one person that could help her through this because she didn't want to take her mother away from Tish during a joyous time - but she had also wanted to be alone, wallowing in self pity.

"Oh Momma." Jina rushed forward into the waiting arms of Alfreah, her mother and best cheerleader. She and Tish were a lot alike. Despite being older than Tish, she felt mothered by her younger sister. Both her sister and mother had a loving-kindness gene that Jina herself felt was missing. Empathy - they had so much of it. Their encouraging nature would have helped a lot, if only she had let them try.

"Why you shun me from coming to hep ya, baby?"

Jina faltered, shaking her head. Her mother wiped her tears. "I didn't." She gave up the false statement at her mother's accusing scrutiny. "I'm sorry, Momma. I gotta get through things, I gotta try. I can't go running to you and Tish every time."

"You don't run to us every time," Alfreah corrected. "And considering all you've been through, I thought you'd have learned ya lesson by now."

Jina nodded. Lessons seemed to need repeating for her to get them: she was either a slow learner or a glutton for punishment, she couldn't be certain which one it was. Her mother had been there for her when Robby was born, though, and she didn't want to deny Tish the same chance with her newborns. Not to mention that even her mother couldn't dig her out of a very large hole, part of which she'd dug on her own. It had been she and Tony but the onus was definitely on her. Marriage and motherhood had tried to soften her, but still hadn't. Her exterior was like steel and she was constantly paying the price for her obtuseness.

"How's Tony and you?" As if reading her mind, her mother raised a tapered gray brow at her. They were the same height, her mother just a tad more bent than her thanks to an achy hip; but they looked into each other's eyes, leveling the truth at one another.

"He's... he's here, downstairs. I made an excuse that I had to go the restroom but I just wanted a few moments with Robby, just to collect myself." Jina wiped at the remaining tears in her eyes. She couldn't wait to see Robby and she couldn't wait to catch up with her mother more. The presence of people who loved her unconditionally was slowly working its magical healing powers on her. She felt somewhat relieved.

"That's good. He wants to be with you," her mother replied.

"He burned the divorce papers," Jina whispered. She hadn't even told Tisha that yet, but she wanted to tell her sister so much, get feedback and just talk to someone. She used to talk to her husband, but it had been sometime since she'd felt at ease doing that.

"Well now, that is even better. Say, he just might get himself back into the family's good graces after a while, now."

Jina laughed. There weren't any others like her family. They all liked Tony well enough, but after the grief he'd caused of late, they didn't even need an explanation to be on her side. They always had her back. Although that was comforting, she nonetheless wanted to protect Tony from the wrath of her family - Jojo's in particular. Tony and Jojo were so much alike, so tough. The thought of protecting Tony was just one of numerous reasons she felt torn. She did love him.

"He loves you, baby. He really does," her mother continued.

"I know Momma, but it's not easy."

"Hush now. We will talk about this, but right now I need to have my tea for the night. Let's not waste time, Tony will be up here any moment. Hey, and when we talk you best not be lying to tell me you're doing better than how I think you're doing, do you hear me?"

"Can't nobody lie to you, Momma." Jina eyed her mother, whose gray hair was still full, vibrant and long. She'd no doubt found a great deal of comfort living with Tisha, buoyed by the rearing - or spoiling, she amended - of her new grandchildren, and Robby for that matter, not to mention a wrap-up of the drama with Dean and Chyna. Another reason Jina had wanted to see her own marital problems and related chaos through alone. The recent year had finally seen a resolution of the issues with her Father's estate over the discrepancy in the bank statements, thanks to Warren and Chauncey Harding. Being finally free from those burdensome events of past, Jina did not need to add her drama again. She was resolute: she'd either work it out or she wouldn't. It was that simple - even though it wasn't simple at all. It was the gist of the situation.

At the children's bedroom door at the end of the hall, there was more light, and Jina scrutinized her mother a bit more closely.

"You look pretty good, Momma."

"Pretty good?" Her mother jumped and grabbed her heart as if shocked. "I beg your pardon?"

Jina laughed. "You know what I mean - you're not so stressed. You think maybe having all your grandchildren around has been good for you?"

Despite what she said, there were some subtle things Jina noticed about her mother. She swallowed, hating to see her Mother age at all, but at the same time thanking God she was aging: better than the alternative, as her mother would often say. Get on in years or get gone in the grave, she would say.

"Of course honey, but I still worry about all my babies, and I always will. And considering - "

"Let's not, Momma." Jina shook her head. "We will talk soon, and I can't wait." Jina smirked: even though she would be grilled for all the information about this and that, there was the good feeling she'd also have unloading to her family the many thoughts and burdensome ideas that ran amuck in her head. As much as she was loath to talk, she knew there was catharsis in sharing what bothered her with those who loved her most. As unsolvable as her issues seemed, just the release of sharing them was therapeutic enough.

Her mother smiled sadly and Jina looked away, gazing around the doorway in which they stood. A soft glow illuminated the frame, and shadows danced as they entered. Stars and moons moved slowly across the walls, likely mesmerizing the children as they dreamed. She didn't expect the place to be so cosmic. It transported her back to the solarium she remembered as a child in science class. It was pretty, and sleep-inducing. It was peace. Despite the guilt that still plagued her about handing her son off to her sister and mother, Jina felt a tiny of bit of reassurance come over her.

"Uh oh, look who is up!" came her mother's voice. "I see you, boy."

Jina dragged her eyes from the dreamscape down to the crib near the door, her mother leaning over to scoop Robby into her arms. Her beautiful child. Having felt good about her choice at first, she was now overcome with emotion. She reached out to take the boy from her mother, with a sigh of relief. Her limbs suddenly felt like jelly; she was unprepared for the weight of him. "Oh my goodness, what have you been eating?"

"He eats just fine," her mother smiled indulgently. "Like a grown man! Hope you got food at home."

Jina looked up, alarmed. The truth was, she didn't have much food at her house at all. Was he eating regular table food? she wondered. What did he like now? Had his palate changed much in the last few weeks?

"I'm just kidding," soothed her mother. "Stop that worrying, I see it in your neck. Nothing to worry about."

"There is... so much, Momma. I feel so bad for abandoning him. I feel horrible."

"Abandoning him? What now? He don't look abandoned to me," retorted her mother. "He look like a healthy baby, eating all he want, playing with his cousins all day long and napping and snacking. I'd say he look like he own all of us. That's what I think - ain't that right, Mr. Robert?"

She tickled the drowsy baby under his chubby chin. "You quit worrying. No abandoning going on round here. Everyone need a break sometime, honey. Now, you sit down here, we will talk later. Now, look how he gone right to sleep. He missed you and he look mighty comfortable in your arms. When he wakes up fully, it'll be like nothing happened. His Momma and Daddy are together and that is all he wants."

Alfreah took a moment to look at Tisha's twins in their own cribs, noting they were still sound asleep. She patted their heads tenderly before turning back to face Jina. "Right now however, listen to me. Babies don't know nothing about guilt trips and blame, not yet. In about ten to twelve years, yes, their manipulative gene will be full throttle. But right now, their love is unconditional. You best get all the kisses and cuddles you can get. Listen: the longer you took, the more determined I grew to come back to Virginia and talk some sense into you. You get this baby back to Virginia, you and Tony get back together and this here child will be bucking up at you and Tony soon enough. You understand me?"

Jina shrugged. "I wish it were that easy."

The mention of Tony just made her feel guilty for sneaking away. Not that he didn't know by now that she was gone. It was just so she could get her bearings - she wasn't at all trying to slight him, in fact she was sure he'd be there any moment. He was never far from her: not in their working marriage times, nor the recent few days into their awkward new we're-divorced-but-living-together times. He always sought her out, sometimes to the point of crowding her, and she couldn't shake him, no matter what. She used to like it, but she'd changed. He'd changed first. Now it just put her on edge.

As her eyes adjusted to the dim light, she noticed the tiny twinkle lights around the base of all three cribs. Three cribs would look crowded in her place, but in this palatial mini-mansion, there was even enough space to put another bed. They could grow into such a room, Tish's twins. There was a room like that at the house in Bethesda, but she'd abandoned it.

Even as dark as it was, this nursery felt inviting: like a play-house, with all the fun stuff, a round rug with the letters of the alphabet circling the numbers in the y center. Two lamps in the shapes of a giraffe and an elephant lit up mobiles over the twins' cribs, a changing table on the other side, the comfy rocking chair covered with a crocheted throw she knew her mom had made, and a mountain of stuffed animals and piles of small, thick picture books - too many to be contained by the tall bookshelf. There was even a mini-fridge in the corner housing a stash of baby food and teddy grahams. Her son loved the cookies, and Tish of course would stock whatever he liked. She needed to make a list herself, she thought again anxiously: see if there were any new items.

"It's only been two weeks," her mother said firmly. "I want you to stop beating yourself up right now."

Jina stared at Robby's sleeping form. Her mother had an uncanny ability to tell how she was feeling at any given moment. So much had happened in the time they'd been apart, and that's what made it so difficult. A lifetime, a life wrecked with the divorce papers, a car accident, learning she was pregnant and a man who she thought wanted a divorce, had no memory and now said he didn't want a divorce, all rushed through her brain.

"It's almost three weeks, ma," she clarified, looking away as her mother gave her the don't-argue-with-me look.

"So what, you the first person ever to need a break?" her mother admonished softly. "Honey, listen. I don't know where my overly confident child has gone, but we got work to do to get her back."

Jina chose to ignore the comment, gently touching the wide-eyed smiling sloth hanging from a tree on the chest of Robby's new pajamas. It had a heart-shaped gray button for a nose. Her boy seemed longer, beefier: it seemed unreal that he was almost a year old now. Even in the dimly lit room, her eyes roved over every inch of him. She caressed his head, but she managed to keep it together. She picked him up again, relishing in the weight of him against her bosom.

"Sit down, there." Her mother pointed. Jina nodded. She belatedly removed her shoes and gingerly took a seat in the rocker. Her mother put the crocheted throw over the two of them and Jina crossed her legs, content just to enjoy the moment for however long it lasted.

"I'll leave you two now." Jina nodded. Her mother stooped to kiss her cheek before exiting.

Jina rocked slowly, the child's head wiggling only slightly in sleep, trying to find a comfortable position before taking a dramatic breath. Her sentiments exactly. She smiled. *Momma is here. I'm never leaving again.* She uttered a quiet prayer aloud for strength, guidance, safety and sound mind for herself and her family, whatever that was going to look like. Before she got to the Amen, she heard Tony's voice saying if for her. When she opened her eyes, there he was, crouched at her feet.

8

Despite his urge to follow Jina as soon as she'd left to find Robby under the guise of a restroom break, Tony remained. He'd planned to make small talk, give Jina a head start. Tish had even asked him privately to give her just a few minutes alone with her son, and he'd agreed. Although he was undeniably growing antsy, he resolved to use the opportunity to pump Tisha for some much-needed intelligence about her sister, his marriage to her, and their rift. He wanted to know it all and hoped to have Tisha as an ally.

Any other time, he wouldn't have sought such information in this underhanded, back-door way - but this was no ordinary time. He wanted to know as much as he could, as fast as we could, so he could be in a better position to resolve their issues and everything else he could control. He tried not to smirk at that word. If this was "control", he'd hate to see what "out of control" looked like. Perhaps the issue was more dire than he thought. Considering he had so little information, anything Tish offered would be like striking gold. But he should have guessed that Tisha was a lot like his wife. Her eyes were kind but scrutinizing. She might have had softer words, she might have been encouraging toward him, but she wasn't going to be free in sharing things that Jina wouldn't later be happy about.

"You must try," she told him. "I think you're willing. Whatever you think it was or wasn't, it was your fault." She smiled sadly at him, skeptical and unsure; maybe even doubtful.

"I am willing. I... I understand," he replied quickly, hoping to reassure her. "But she could... just..."

Tish held up a hand. "Would-a-could-a-should-a won't help you now. That's water under the bridge. To be blunt, surviving this accident means you're not done."

Tony nodded. He knew he had done something, and considering his accident and his current status with Jina, he knew he wasn't going to get any help from Tish just yet. She shook her head, a smile of apology on her face. He nodded. He couldn't blame her. He knew that he was the bad guy, then and for the foreseeable future. He stood, ready to go find Jina, and was suddenly wrapped in a tight hug that gave him some much-needed encouragement.

The trek up the stairs felt like climbing a mountain. He was weighed down by the lack of information on his memory or his past, and still more apprehensive about seeing his son. He had been at that house before, he knew, but even as he trekked down the hall, he didn't feel any fresh memories assault him since he'd had the revelation about his child.

He was thankful that he remembered, but it still blew his mind that he could ever forget something so significant, even temporarily. The more he gained, the more he marveled at the human mind, even if he was presently angry about its ability to be so complex and forget the things his he knew deep down in his heart, like the love he felt for his wife. He reflected that he'd never really dealt with the pain of losing other children with Jina. That was a locker he'd hope to cement shut. The grief was real, but not dealing with it couldn't be good.

Entering the room, he was still at first, rooted in the doorway. He heard Jina's soft voice, praying words as she rocked their son back and forth. He moved as quietly as he could, noticing the other two babies sleeping peacefully in their respective cribs. He crouched down before her, saddened that they hadn't been praying together and that he'd missed this which felt like a significant beginning. The sight of her seemed familiar and foreign to him all at the same time.

Jina glanced up, startled to find him at her feet.

"I can't leave him again." She stood with Robby in her arms. "He's gotten bigger." She paused.

"You can't leave us again." She didn't face him as she whispered the words. Though he was taken aback by what she said, he placed a hand on her shoulder, wanting to embrace her fully.

"I won't," Tony replied simply. "Let's take him to our room for a little bit." It was as if he read her mind: she had stopped at the crib, as if waiting for permission to do just as he suggested. She hugged him tighter, then shot down the hall ahead of him. Tony checked the girls, still unbothered by the whispered banter, before hastily closing the door almost all the way and following her.

Right on cue, Tish approached him in the hallway. He made a mental note of the door that Jina had entered before focusing on Tish. "Um, hey…"

"Hello. Hey, I think it's a good idea if you and Jina spend some time alone with Robby, so I'm gonna take the girls out tomorrow and you'll have the place to yourselves. Does that sound OK?"

Tony nodded eagerly. "I know that Jina wants to spend time with you all too, though," he added.

Tish shrugged. "We'll just be gone for a few hours - we do live here, remember, so we'll be fine. I - uh, Jina never remembers to pack her hair care products or pajamas, so… well, here's some hair stuff I like. Maybe you can put it on for her."

"Me?" he asked, startled.

"Yes," Tish smiled, "and then if she needs pajamas I have some of those too. Tell her to text me - or she could always borrow your shirt." Tish smiled craftily.

"Uh, uh, okay."

Tony took the small jar of hair product, not quite following the subtle smile that she gave him. He didn't know if she was trying to drop hints about laying on the charm or really suggesting some new products for Jina to try. He knew women were particular about their hair, but it just seemed odd that Tish would be giving him the suggestions to relay rather than giving them directly to Jina. He backed away down the hall, giving up on deciphering whatever clues he wasn't getting.

When he entered the room, he was surprised to see that Robby was in Jina's arms. They both seem ready for bed. The child seemed somewhat awake and semi-interested in the fact that his mother was present. Sleepy eyes followed Tony as he entered and set the jar on the bare dresser. Jina was in a pair of shorts, but still wore the cotton shirt she'd been traveling in all day. She let out a sigh. "Oh - I forgot my pajama tops. I managed the bottom of course but I can never keep the pairs together."

"Uh, it's ok, you can wear my shirt," said Tony, a little awkwardly.

"Just give me the one you have," she answered. "I'll take a shower in the morning."

Suddenly understanding what Tish might have meant by their brief exchange back in the hallway, Tony only hesitated moments before unbuttoning his outer shirt and removing the crisp white undershirt he had on underneath to hand over. Standing, Jina handed Robby to him before entering the bathroom. He heard water run, followed by the whir of the electric toothbrush. Tony concentrated on his drowsy son, alone with him for the first time. He leaned over him, kissing him tenderly on the cheek and staring into eyes that stared back at him for only snatches of time before closing fully. "You're gonna come home with us, tomorrow or the next day," Tony murmured. "We got this - you, me and Mommy. It won't ever change."

Just then, Jina exited the bathroom, wearing only his shirt and the skimpy pajama shorts. The sudden strength of the desire he felt caught him by surprise. Trying to focus on his child again, he laid him down carefully in the center of the bed before springing quietly up again to busy himself. Jina smiled faintly.

"Sorry, I should have remembered my clothes."

"It's fine." He cleared his throat. "It's fine," he repeated. "I... I like it."

When she climbed gingerly onto the bed, she scratched her head and Tony remembered the grease that Tish had given him. Seizing the little jar from the dresser, he came up cautiously behind her. "Uh, Tish said you might like this..."

She took it from his hands, read the ingredients, opened it and took a deep sniff.

"Oh my God, it smells so good," she exclaimed. He leaned in and she tilted it to him where he also sniffed. "Mmmm, like something to eat," he agreed.

She laughed, closing the jar again.

"Aren't you going to try it?"

Jina shook her head. "I'm kind of tired. I'll just steal it from her. She knows better than to give me stuff just to try."

Taking the jar back, Tony opened it, scooping a little onto his fingers and rubbing it on the tips of her hair. "Let me see here... how hard can it be?"

"Um..."

"Shh," he admonished before climbing up onto the bed. He settled himself behind her and before she could protest, he used his ungreased fingers to part her hair from back to front, starting at the nape of her neck, dotting her scalp with the gel as he went along. When he was finished, he gently parted her hair in much the same way, from ear to ear, and repeated the ministrations. With a final small scoop, he used both fingers to massage the oil throughout. Though through the first few touches she'd been tense, she relaxed as he went along, easing back against his chest and leaning her head more and more into his hands.

He liked the feeling of her thick hair in his hands, and he pushed his fingers deep into her scalp, rubbing in a steady circular motion all over her head, until she was drifting off into sleep. He continued even as she nodded off against him. The weight of her body felt good against his chest. Considering they had yet to be intimate since his accident, a part of him wanted to believe it would happen again, and soon. His nostrils grazed her collar bone, before planting a soft kiss there. That startled her awake.

She looked back at him and he could have sworn the desire he felt right then had snuck up on her too. He couldn't tell for sure; he only hoped it was there somewhere. Her eyes quickly moved past him, seeking the child that slept unawares next to them. "We should put him in his crib," she whispered.

"How about he stays with us tonight?"

The moment somewhat gone, Tony rubbed the excess grease onto his own baldhead before replacing the jar on the nightstand and climbing off the bed to retrieve Robby and pull back the comforter. Jina scooted into her side of the bed, drawing Robby closer into her side and pulling the covers up halfway before laying down to face the child, and Tony, when he climbed in on the other side.

"What if this is habit-forming?" she wondered aloud.

Tony turned and shrugged. "There are worse things in life. Plus, as soon as we are together in… every way, he's gotta go. I'll have no problem giving him an eviction notice."

She smirked. "Are you even thinking about that?"

"Have you *been* here the last ten minutes?" he challenged quickly. He paused. "Are – are you?"

She waited a beat before answering. "The head message was nice... thank you."

He nodded. "To answer your question - "

"Don't. Goodnight." Jina reached over and abruptly snapped off the bedside lamp.

Despite her pretending to go right to sleep, Tony stared at the ceiling and continued to talk. His voice was low, but he knew she listened as she opened her eyes again. There was only a small night-light: since he was unfamiliar with this room, he didn't want to bump his toe in the night, plus with Robby present he thought it was best to keep it on. It pained him briefly that he didn't remember whether or not his only child was afraid of the dark. It was the same pain he felt when he realized that he couldn't remember his favorite food, nor Jina's for that matter. It was the little things that served up the most painful reminders of all he had lost and had yet to find.

Dismissing the as-yet-unfound rooms of his memory, he turned on his side to face her again. "Yes, I'm thinking about that and so much more. Now, just moments ago, I was thinking about you in that way," he emphasized. "And I've thought about... that, since the day you walked out of my hospital room. Even while I was in pain, I wanted you very much."

"It's a natural thing, it's just human nature," she said dismissively.

The time ticked by and they seemed to stare at each other for an hour. Jina was still staring at him, maybe even daring him to say more. She fought her massage-induced sleepiness from earlier, and he fought the urge not to lay on all the charm and finally give her the kind of kiss that would kindle the fire of being with his wife in an intimate way once again.

"Human nature, natural, yes, all of that - with about ten times the voltage of desire and what seems like an eternity since our last time," Tony continued. "But when you say the word, Jina, make no mistake."

"Soon," she whispered and he was surprised. He was right about her and all that he guessed she thought about. Despite the uncertainty of everything, they were on the same page.

He nodded, smiling, before he sat up on his elbow and leaned in to kiss her. At last, she turned her face to his. "Not soon enough, but I'll take it," he said. After kissing her twice, he kissed Robby good night, then settled in for another night of torture as he waited patiently for the rest of his life and his memories to move forward.

9

What began as a peaceful night's rest, induced by the thoughts that his family was reunited, was interrupted - rather early, he guessed from the darkness - by a little someone working their way up onto his chest and smacking him solidly in the face. Tony felt the tug on the covers, heard the determined baby huffing noises, then the slap told him it was time to move. "All right, all right," he smiled groggily at Robby, whispering that they be quiet and not wake Mommy.

He dressed quickly and quietly, donning a casual shirt and a pair of jogging pants, then kissed Jina, whispering that he was going downstairs with Robby and would see about getting them something to eat. At the top of the stairs in the large house, he noticed the pictures lining the wall as he descended with the child in tow. He thought back to the house in Bethesda. While he'd seen a picture of its massive exterior before heading to Jina's tiny apartment, he wondered if it were as big as this house. Did he feel comfortable there?

Not without Jina, his mind reminded him. He wouldn't feel comfortable without her anywhere. The apartment was small, and though he didn't remember the large house in contrast, he knew he'd been from modest and rather humble beginnings in New York's slum neighborhood. He and his Mom had each other back then, and that was all he needed. As determined as he felt about getting his memory back, a part of him enjoyed shunning material possessions and wealth. As he uncovered more about himself and his past, especially about getting back with his father in his life, he hoped that humility had been the one thing about him that hadn't changed. *You were driving a car that hasn't been released, hot off the manufacturer's assembly line before it crashed and burned up,* his mind reminded him. True, but it still felt odd. Maybe whatever vehicle he drove normally – a Ford Escape? A Honda perhaps? - was in the shop or something. He laughed. Another hole to figure out.

When he entered the kitchen, he saw Tish there smiling. "I see that despite having his mommy and daddy back the human alarm clock still reigns supreme, huh, Robby?" Tish smiled at Tony, giving his shoulder a touch before kissing the baby, who giggled at her. "You can put him in the high chair if you want," she continued. "He knows the drill."

"Uh, thanks. Good morning - how is everyone?" He directed his greeting to Chase, who sat at the table holding one of his infant daughters. The other was looking around curiously from a table-top bassinet.

"All good," Chase answered. "Hungry bunch of women in here, man, but good. Oh, and little men, of course."

"Little, really?" Tony said with a skeptical smile.

As he belted Robby into the chair and snapped on the plastic tray, the child, fully awake now, pounded his open palms in frustration, laughing at Chase and the girls.

"See what I mean?" Tish said with a laugh, turning to dump out a bowl of cut soft fruit and a heap of cheerios on Robby's tray, which he commenced to grab by the handful and shove all that he could muster into his mouth.

Tony stood watching, amazed at how much his son had changed.

"Since Jina is sleeping, I thought I could just, uh, ask a few questions about some things?" he began. He stood back, hoping they'd be open to answering a few things without too much alarm. Chase and Tish exchanged looks.

"Is that wise? What did your doctor say?" countered Tish, handing him a steaming cup.

"Um, uh, thanks." Tony took the proffered coffee and busied himself doctoring it at the counter. *What did his doctor say?* That was a good question. He honestly hadn't listened, and he certainly hadn't made a plan to follow up, so focused on his goal as he'd been: intent on exiting the hospital and finding his wife. He hadn't thought to hear anything from his doctor at all, except possibly an ETA on his memory returning - and his doctor couldn't possibly know the answer to that.

"I think it will be okay," he went on carefully. "It can't hurt, right? I know you're likely not wanting to upset Jina by telling me anything, but if it's any constellation to you, I want my marriage and life back. Look, whatever I did or said, wrong as it might have been, there must have been a reason. Pieces, whatever you can give me, will help me get there a little bit faster and that's all I want."

Tish stood back, eyeing him skeptically. "Have you been back to work with your father?"

At first it seemed like a strange question, but he pressed on anyway. Did his work and his father play a role?

"Uh, no, but that's the weird thing to me too," he answered. "I mean, why on earth would I accept anything from him? I really disliked him, I remember that much. I can't see taking anything from him - and to find out I actually work for him?"

Tish nodded. "It was odd to all of us. It was always a bone of contention: the hours you worked, that guy - your partner, Keith?"

"Yes, Keith. Keith Munrow, is it?" he queried.

"Seems like you had something to prove to your father," Chase weighed in. "The Keith person isn't the best or most objective character."

"Really?"

Tish nodded. "And that car?" she added. "At first those things didn't seem important to you, and then before we knew what was up you were accepting a limited-or-first-edition, whatever it was."

"I mean it was nice, though, you sent me some pictures," Chase put in.

"Really?" Tony said

"Yeah," Chase said, reaching for his phone. Tony was about to step forward when Tish cut him a look that resembled fire darts. Chase stopped reaching for his phone and the men's momentary shared excitement over the vehicle ceased. Chastened, Chase looked down at his child, adjusting the bottle and giving Tony a silent shrug of the shoulder.

Tish landed the fiery eyes back on Tony and he took a step back. "Really? It nearly killed you," Tish admonished. "Poor Jina: giving up her baby to me, then nearly losing you. You know it nearly killed her? Do you even understand, Tony?"

Tony was silent as his thoughts turned to Jina. "Yeah," he said gruffly, searching for the questions he needed to pose next. "I'm... I'm sorry."

"Do they have any leads on what caused the vehicle crash?" Chase asked.

"No," answered Tony. "I should be speaking with the detective again soon, but it looks like the vehicle has some proprietary issues so they are doing their own investigation on it."

Tish raised an eyebrow. "Sounds a little suspect, doesn't it?"

"It was a limited edition, as you said. But if whomever is doing the investigation sees the engine and all that's there, that could be duplicated by investors or competitors, people out to steal some information," Chase added. He sneaked a look at his wife, clearly hoping to win brownie points for the idea.

"Sensitive information?" Tony whispered. He was now thinking about the car more extensively that he had before. Truth be told, he hadn't thought anything of it: he had dismissed his accident altogether, chalking it up to a fancy new car with all the bells and whistles he didn't really know how to operate. Never had he considered that there might be something deeper. When he had been extracted from the vehicle, his back hurting more than he cared to admit, he had just been thankful to be alive, even as the ambulance worked to get him out of the twisted metal, he'd blanked out from the pain, and only recalled waking up seeing his doctor and Jina standing next to his bedside. To poke around any more on the car front seemed misdirected, somehow.

"Whatever the case is, you should have never let him talk you into accepting it," Tish said firmly. "That's part of the problem: Keith always coming around. Tony, you have to protect your marriage at all costs."

She covered a sheet with strips of bacon and placed it in the oven. Every single piece of information brought about a thousand questions, making his brain hurt. He considered what they said. When he and Jina had spoken about this very subject, he'd thought they were talking about his father as the guilty party: the one who had talked him into accepting the exorbitant gift, or at least thinking about keeping it - he remembered something about that, some argument. If it had been a gift from his father, he didn't know what Jina had meant about Keith's involvement. He was confused.

"Listen, wait, my father gave me that car, right?

"Yes, I think so - to buy your affection no doubt – but..."

"Wait, okay, who are you saying talked me into it? Into what, exactly?"

"Into driving it," Tish replied. "It was that Keith Munroe

guy. He was pushing you to take it out on the worst night. Oh Tony, there was some kind tornado watch that day: torrential rains, flooding, what a nightmare. We heard about it on the news way down here – I remember we were worried about you guys still up there, Jojo and Dean and Chyna too. I tell you, that night was - "

The words died on Tish's lips when a loud thump just inside the hallway startled all of them. Nearest to the entrance, Tony was first to back up and out of the kitchen and to see Jina picking herself up from the floor at the bottom of the stairs.

"Jina, did you fall? Are you all right?"

He moved quickly to her where she lay, his hands reaching out to help her up; but she barely acknowledged him, rushing into the kitchen, not slowing until she reached the chair where Robby sat shoveling his last handfuls of cereal into his mouth. Tony moved cautiously to stand beside her, alarmed by her erratic behavior as he watched the scene unfold.

Jina hastily patted the boy's head before leaning in to plant a kiss on his brow, then left the room as quickly as she had entered, muttering "excuse me" under her breath. She headed for the den, with Tish and Tony in hot pursuit. There she sat down heavily on the leather sofa and cried into her hands.

10

"We are just chatting. We are chatting, okay? Nothing is wrong. Did you have a bad dream?" Tish asked as she sat down beside her. Unwillingly at first, Jina's head went into her sister's arms. A shoulder hugging her close, her head laying on her shoulder, she took a deep cleansing breath. Tony kneeled in front of her, placing his hands tentatively on her knees. Jina immediately closed her eyes, hating the way he looked at her.

Thinking about everything that had happened in the span of a few days was a rollercoaster. There had been the calm scene of last night: the people she cared for most all under one roof and, for the first time in a month, her husband and son in the same bed with her, safe, unharmed, uninjured. That's how she went to bed, but that wasn't how she woke up. For a few moments upon waking, the disorienting unfamiliarity of the space and her absent child had sent her into a full-blown panic. She couldn't wake up fully as she fumbled among the covers finding no one, feeling increasingly stifled: like she couldn't breathe. She no longer had her baby or her husband by her side. She would take the new version of him, as painful as that was, buoyed only by the fact that there were pieces of the old him still discernable - pieces that made her forget anything had transpired at all. She tried to hold onto those now, but as she turned and tossed in her bed, it felt as if they too slipped away in the darkness, just out of her grasp, because of some stranger looming on the horizon but too far away for her to see.

Though she hadn't seen the crash that injured Tony, she did see the resulting mangled mess on the television. She thought she'd lost. She was lost. Air whooshed from her lungs as she uttered a strangled cry: her child slipping from her hands, her hands reaching, frantically encountering emptiness. She managed to wrench herself awake, irrationally annoyed now by everything around her that was not familiar: the empty sheets, the early light piercing the dimness of the room. She'd hauled herself up off the bed, the covers tangling around her feet as she kicked them off to go in search of her son. Running down the stairs, she fell, causing more potential injury to her unborn child - which also made her so angry. Hearing the voices in the kitchen had brought her around at last, realizing that there was no danger: that everyone, including Robby, was fine. And then, yes, she was embarrassed. Her family would find her crazy, weird: as if she were having some kind of nervous breakdown. Considering how she acted, she wasn't sure she could fault them for whatever they thought about her mental state. Her child was clearly fine, wanting for nothing and enjoying his food with his Aunt and Uncle.

"Jina, baby?"

Opening her eyes, she snatched her hand away from him, pushing herself deeper into the leather cushions of the sofa. Tish was hovering before her, staring her in the eye. "We're all right here - right here."

Jina hated the way her sister looked at her: with concern, with questions, with pity.

"Don't look at me like that."

"I'm looking at you, and I see you," Tish responded gently. "I want you tell me what happened just now. What scared you?"

Jina looked down at herself, belatedly noting that she was still in her skimpy shorts. She was so embarrassed.

"How about some water? Tony, a glass of water please?"

Jina watched Tony hesitate to move from her side, but eventually he acquiesced, standing to his full height and leaving the room.

With him gone, Tish's voice was much more stern that it had been.

"You gonna tell me if your nightmares are starting up again? And you need to tell Tony, too. The stress of everything is catching up with you and he needs to support you, but he can't do that if he doesn't know."

"No, no, I just, forgot where I was for a second," she whispered, hoping Tony didn't hear. "Yeah, I just... had a nightmare. It felt unbelievably real." She tried to rub the sleep from her eyes, but every time she closed them, the faceless man was there.

Tony returned with the water and handed to her. "Thanks," she said taking it from him and downing it, slowing the last few gulps lest she throw it all back up. He took it from her shaky fingers and placed it on the nearby table.

"Dreams scare us," Tish went on. "They seem real, but they are not. They do come out of some kind of fear, though. So let's get to it, Jina. Why don't you, uh, tell us what your nightmare was about? Was it about Robby?"

She nodded, as tears came to her eyes immediately."Robby was gone. I was trying to hold on to him, he was gone."

"You saw him, he's fine," soothed her sister.

"I know that."

"Okay, who took him in the dream, then?"

"I couldn't see his face, I don't-I don't know." She turned, casting her stormy, frustration filled eyes once again on Tony. She hesitated, with Tony there on the floor kneeling at her side. She needed a minute to exit her nightmare, collect herself and return to normal. She looked at him warily, hating the confusion she saw in his eyes.

Tony's hand reached out to hers. Rather than pull away, this time she let him pry them apart, working them in his own, willing her to look at him.

"You used to have nightmares, when you were stressed and after..."

Jina's eyes bulged in shock that he might remember. The thing was, *she* didn't want to remember that particular time. She'd done a lot of work and counseling to come out of that.

"That's right." Tish nodded eagerly, encouraging him, while shooting her sister a cross look. Maybe if she only related a little, he might remember the rest on his own. Encouraging his memory to return was, bottom line, something she should have been able to do. The part that was hard for Jina was the fear that he would then remember everything, including why he'd asked her for a divorce.

"Can you excuse us?" Jina asked Tish. Surprised, Tish nodded. "You can trust him," she added softly.

Jina nodded. She was afraid of the vulnerability she felt, not to mention that with her sister gone, she'd have to answer his questions all by herself. That was the scary part.

When Tish exited, Tony took her sister's place behind Jina. He rubbed her back gently and nuzzled her neck.

"I can't stand that you don't trust me," he murmured. "Hey - I'm here with you, alone," Jina protested. "I trust you."

Tony made a face. "In front of your sister, you hesitated. And so yes, you trust me with your physical safety, but I'm talking about your thoughts: do you trust me with what is going through your mind, or in here?" He pointed a finger at her chest. "Whatever those bad thoughts are, I can handle them."

"I can't even handle them, and they're my dreams. How can you?" she shot back.

"Try me."

"I don't even know what they are, except for the faceless man taking things away from me," she admitted.

"Keith?"

Jina recoiled. "Where did that come from? No, I don't - I don't think so. I don't know."

She would fight that Keith with all she had. She found him a nuisance, a selfish jerk, a workaholic, maybe even a crook and a shyster.

"Tish and Chase said that you started to dislike him."

"And you already know that part," she reminded.

"Yes, but is he responsible for our rift?" he begged.

"Partly," Jina allowed slowly. "Him, your work, your father's work; then your wacky step mother and this inexplicable loyalty you have to your father, out of nowhere all of sudden, in this last year."

"The person in the dream, he took Robby?"

"Yes."

"Where was I?" he questioned.

"I don't know. Hurt, injured, at work?"

"How many times have you had this dream?"

She shrugged. "I have different ones. They started back near your accident, before I mitigated them with journaling and counseling. It's like – well, knowing that Robby is back in my care and, I just feel inept."

"You're not."

"I know. Logically, I know. I would die to save him, that's one of the reasons he's even here; but I need better stress coping mechanisms. Maybe I even need to do something about my diet."

"We did eat kind of late last night," Tony conceded.

"And it was fun! It's so great here with my sister, the girls, my Mom."

"We should move here," he said.

Jina's head snapped up. "What?"

"We'll come back to that," he smiled, "but now, your dreams, back to them. You had them in college, after, something?"

"Do you remember?"

She felt so confused by him. Was he even serious? She shook her head, eyeing him skeptically, surprised that his memory went all the way back to college.

"Yes, tell me." Tony drew closer, putting his arm around her.

She hesitated but hated to think about that time: she had tried so hard to forget it. "After I was assaulted," she eventually said.

She could feel Tony's entire body tense. The hand lying across the back of the sofa clenched tightly into a fist before relaxing.

"Why don't I know who that was? Why didn't he pay for what he did?" he growled.

"They never found out who did it. Look, there is something I haven't told you this entire week - two things, actually. From after your accident."

"Okay, tell me now." Tony moved closer, forcing her around to face him but never loosening his embrace. He leaned back to search her eyes. Jina swallowed.

"That... that I thank God you're okay. That I didn't lose you."

"Is that all?"

Jina gaped. "That's kind of huge, don't you think? I don't want God to think I'm ungrateful. As jacked as our relationship was, I never wanted to die."

"That's a relief. Thank you. But meanwhile, sounds like I made a stupid decision to accept a new car that's not even in full production yet - some rare elite model, just because my father bought it for me. He probably did it as some kind of peace offering to make up for the years he abandoned my Mom and me. Jina, I'm glad you're okay, but the more information I gather, the more I think I don't deserve any of it. The way I see it, I have a second chance to get this right and to finally find out what the hell is going on - why I changed into a person I don't recognize. I have to admit, there are parts I don't want to know, because they still don't fit."

"I see pieces of the old you," Jina replied softly. "You're different, although you're still the man I fell in love with. It's the gaps in your memory that hang over me: why you rejected us, why you wanted a divorce in the first place."

"I don't."

"I know you don't, or you think you don't. It's on hold, whatever, okay. Fine."

"But what else is there to tell me?" Tony pressed.

There was a pause.

"I'm pregnant."

"What?"

She hadn't been prepared for the tears to come so quickly to his eyes. She looked away to keep her own tears at bay. Regardless of how he felt, she was happy. Whatever he thought, she wanted her children and this one growing inside of her was a blessing she thought she'd never have again.

"Jina."

"Stop, stop. Don't cry please," she pleaded. "I can't deal with a grown-ass man crying. I'm happy, sorta. I mean, I'm happy I'm pregnant."

"You can't possibly think I'm not happy?"

Jina looked away. His response should have soothed her own tortured thoughts but it didn't. It just made her more confused.

"You were always mean as hell about men showing emotion," Tony smiled through his tears. "I know you, and I still love all of it, so you go ahead and dish it out - but tell me this, why keep it from me? I am so happy for us. Whatever deranged thoughts you have in your head, rest assured that I want you *and* my children."

Her head whipped around so fast that both her neck and her brain hurt.

"Because…"

His face darkened. "Because what, Jina?"

Jina managed to slip out of his embrace. The den had a small window facing the back yard and she stared out, thinking about how beautiful it was. She could play with her children there, as Tish might with the girls as soon as they could walk, and as she might've done with Thomas before he became too cool for all that and exchanged playtime for video games. Seeing the wide open spaces and the tall weeping Georgia oak tree made her wish she hadn't left her Bethesda home, now that she had another child on the way. Comparisons were starting to creep in. Where would they play? Was the house under contract? Was it even worth trying to get back? Could they afford it? She felt unprepared; her entire future seemed so uncertain right then. She wished she could know so much more than she did.

"Are you going to answer me, Jina?"

She started. "Because what scares me about my nightmares and visions and all is that *you asked* for the divorce. You put our house on the market, you started packing up our life. You changed, and now you're back, you burned the divorce papers, and I'm so confused. The scariest thing of all is that, as hard as I try to unmask the masked person, to uncover my monster, is that sometimes I think..."

"What?"

Jina took a deep breath. "I sometimes think the person taking the things I love away from me... is you."

11

Are you gonna be all right? Jina recalled the words her sister had said as they prepared to leave Macon and return to Virginia - after she'd managed to take a shower, don real clothes and reemerge downstairs looking more like the sane person she usually was, despite having exhibited behavior to the contrary earlier that morning. Having the terrifying experience of her fear being exposed and confronted was the only way to get past it, she knew.

For now, they all sat down to Tish's heavenly breakfast and managed good conversation. It was good to catch up with her mother, Thomas, and the twin girls, who were getting bigger and bigger every day. Jina already couldn't wait to see them again.

Tony, as shocked as he was about what she'd said about her thoughts of him and particularly the role he played in her dream, had listened thoughtfully, without taking visible offense. She knew the dream wasn't true, and his reassurances helped, but her dream and what she thought she might have seen were still powerfully influential on her thoughts. She knew she couldn't be sure of anything really, and she accepted that. What she could control was whether she took Tony at his word, going by what he continued to show her and what she felt. She loved him, and that would have to suffice. Together, they were determined to figure it all out, taking it one day at a time. They talked a lot more on the drive back home than they had during the tense drive down. Perhaps they were both relieved that they had at least some sense of normalcy now that they had Robby in their care. They were together to co-parent, whatever that looked like, and there was reassurance in that alone. Whatever happened, she resolved to take her sister's advice to be kind to everyone, especially to Tony - and to herself.

Traveling with a small child in tow this time, however, wasn't exactly ideal. Jina thanked God that they'd taken the car rather than flying. Sometimes they both found themselves comically yelling over the babbling child, who heroically managed to stay awake for most of the trip and used his growing vocabulary to entertain them. Most of it was gibberish, with actual words thrown in here and there: mostly 'no' and 'yes'. Jina didn't want Robby using headphones just yet, trying to avoid any premature hearing loss by setting things at a normal tone for him to watch aloud on her cell phone.

Jina sat in the back sometimes, and Tony managed more of the long drive than she had thought was a good idea; but before long, there they were back in Virginia, staring at a vast mound of boxes and grocery bags. Somehow, with frequent trips back and forth with the overflowing trolley cart, things were slowly but surely getting put away in the right places.

They'd gone just a little overboard at the Baby Depot: likely a symptom of their own parental guilt getting the best of them. Thinking a little guiltily about all the new stuff plus the old stuff, she set about getting Robby out of his car seat. Once standing, he looked around cautiously while holding onto her knee, as if deciding what to explore first. Jina was comforted by the fact that he held on to her. At least he had stayed there for a few nights previously. The fact remained that she had sent her son away in order to unpack as much as she could, to focus on the move. Though she was worried about him adjusting, for the last hour he had seemed just fine.

Tony returned and dramatically fell to the floor, sprawled out amongst bags tossed this way and that. Jina smiled. His dramatic splat mirrored her own exhaustion.

"There was at least one last empty chair to sit in, sir: considering your back, the floor isn't the best place," she chided him. "Chase is not here to help you up here, remember, and I'm flagged out."

Seizing an opportunity, Robby moved quickly toward him, mounting his Daddy's chest as he liked to do.

"Don't you dare!" Jina admonished, surprised by her own voice. She knew exactly what he was about to do. The child looked over laughing, but did obediently put his hand down.

"He knows I deserve it," Tony smiled. He closed his eyes and opened them to look at her. "What's the matter?"

"Nothing. I was just... thinking about my dream."

"Don't."

"You thought I was crazy, didn't you?"

Tony gave her a look. "I would never think that, because you're not."

She nodded, unconvinced, but she wanted to move on. If the dreams were recurring, she'd know soon enough. She looked around at all the stuff. Robby jumped up and down on Tony's chest, and she smiled at the sight.

"So, we went a little crazy - no pun intended - today at the store," she clarified. "Can we at least agree that we won't let our relationship guilt-stuff spoil him quite so much in the future?"

Tony nodded. "It was fun, though, you have to admit," he grinned. "We did something together as a family and I had fun. We should do more of it." He stood up and began putting some of the items away, gathering bags and boxes as he emptied the car and gradually stacked up the plentiful loot, setting Robby down so he could roam.

Jina sat, just staring. The shopping spree was getting the best of her: a nap sounded really good, but it was also approaching evening and she should eat first. Tony was right: it had been nice to shop, to push Robby around in cart and do a familial and normal things they hadn't done in some time. Not to mention that Tony had also picked up lots of food, fresh produce and greens, which meant she was also going to eat really well for the foreseeable future. He knew the truth about everything now, so she didn't have to work so hard to hide anymore. Not that she could've hidden for much longer: she was getting bigger all the time, so soon the jig would've been up anyway. Ready to see what he would make for dinner, Jina stood.

"Tony, you're in great shape. Surviving the crash was probably a testament to your physical athleticism."

"So what do I do: jog, weight-lifting, what?"

"Boxing," she answered firmly.

"Boxing, really?"

Jina nodded. "You were a fighter when I met you. Lightweight regional champion. Here, let me help unpack some things - let's get this place in shape before we see about dinner."

"No lifting," Tony reminded her. "I'll do it. You just keep an eye on Robby."

He embraced her, placing a hand on her belly. He kissed her: she would have to get used to leaning in. She didn't want her own desires to get the best of her, so she felt a little restrained, a little uncertain. Everything seemed so new and foreign, yet familiar, all at the same time.

She lifted her face and his lips hovered above hers before planting fleeting kisses on her mouth and forehead.

"What else are you doing since you quit the paper?" he queried.

"Blogging," she answered hesitantly. "I had a blog about grief and loss. It's grown quite a large following, but I've put it down in the last month. I'm thinking I need to get back to it. Oh, and I didn't quit the paper, you know. I was fired."

"For what?"

She paused. "I left an anonymous tip about Senator Gary Williams - that's my brother's wife's ex-husband - to get his book canceled."

Tony shrugged. "I'm sure you had good reason."

"It wasn't right, whatever the reason was. I was glad for the firing, but I should have done something different. It only proved that what you think is anonymous, isn't."

"Was there any fallout?"

"Sure. He was mad. I don't know if he ever knew the truth. I also doubt Chyna and Dean know exactly how the book got canceled, and I want to keep it like that. It saved her – them - so much grief. Their relationship with the senator and a business mogul was a mess. It turned out that the Hardigs' were just doing their bidding. The son was after Chyna. He later committed suicide, after a sting operation in which he admitted to trying to kill my brother and burn down his office and his house."

"That sounds pretty heavy," agreed Tony. "There was someone else too, right? A woman?"

Jina nodded. "Lisa Stephens. She came on to you before all this went down. I hated her guts." She pulled away. She didn't really think he and Lisa had done anything, but she hadn't ever been quite sure. She was relieved when Tony brought the subject back to the original theme.

"Where's the senator now?" he asked.

"He's on parole for the next ten years. He was accused of rape and misuse of campaign funds."

"Shouldn't some of that exonerate you?" asked Tony, incredulously. "Looks like it was true. Whatever you did might have set things in motion."

"It doesn't exonerate me. I'm glad he was brought to justice, I'm glad the book was cancelled - that he couldn't put out something so full of lies just to hurt the people I love - but I shouldn't have done it that way."

Tony nodded. Although Jina had so much judgment for herself, she couldn't say that she felt any from him.

"We've all done something we're not proud of," he reminded her gently. "If the end result was him going to jail and you had nothing to do with that investigation except to point out something that might have been true anyway, you should give yourself a break, Jina. Now, what's next? Do you wish to return to a newspaper or something along those lines?"

Jina sighed. "I may have to, the money I saved may run out in a year. We were gonna split the money from the house, but I don't know what's happening with that.

"Did you want that house?"

She hesitated. "I don't know. I want peace of mind, stability and my family more than anything. With a second child on the way, it's going to get crowded here. I don't want the kids to share rooms forever. I shared a room with Tish and it was fine, we were close and we were both girls, but it would be nice for this one to have their own space eventually."

"Do you know if it's a he or a she?" he asked.

"No. Not yet." She held her belly tenderly as she closed her eyes.

"What do you want?"

"A healthy, live birth," she said simply, closing her eyes and focusing on the subtle sounds her body made when she tuned everything else out.

Tony nodded and embraced her again.

"Your family is and will continue to be intact. We can make it here or move by the time baby number two is a year old. I'll see what's going on with the house and I'll fix it, all of it."

"I... I don't know what I want," she admitted. "Some of my recent decisions have been wrong, or at least not easy and maybe not the best. I felt hasty and overwhelmed, and that's not the best way to make decisions; not to mention this baby is going to have me just as hormonal as ever. I apologize in advance for what I have said and what I still might say. But about the house, the money, all of it. I think about the money that we didn't have for IVF and fertility treatments. We even spent a few grand to vet a couple of surrogates we weren't even sure about; then there was the house, the boat, all of that. If we'd just have been patient and waited on God to bless us in His own time."

"Sometimes God says to move forward with things," returned Tony firmly. "Many families have gone the routes we chose only to end up with two children, one biological and one adopted, or acquired in another way."

She nodded. "But so much waste. It strained us, Tony, and now we're in this tiny place and it's only just enough."

"When did we make love?"

She was surprised at the turn of questioning. She smiled shyly. "Maybe a week before your accident?"

"Were we going to reconcile?"

She didn't know then, and some parts of her suggested she still had no idea. She felt like they were, only he hadn't mentioned it. In fact, up until he burned the divorce decree right before her very eyes, she hadn't been sure.

"Maybe." She shrugged her shoulders in defeat.

"What we did just shows how wrong it was for us - for me - to even have thought about divorce. I wasn't done then, and I'm still not ever going to be done with our relationship."

"As great as it has been in the bedroom, sex does not equate being able to make a lasting marriage," she reminded him.

"It wasn't just sex for me. It was love."

She nodded. Talking about this and her feeling sleepy after

a long day wasn't helping matters. Her hormones raged at the thought of him.

"I want us to get rid of everything that made us lose sight of what was important," she resolved. "We can get a house like my Mom's or a three bedroom. We don't need all of it, okay?"

Tony nodded. "I'm more clear than ever now on what's important."

She nodded and, releasing her belly, reached out to embrace him. Robby wanted in, ambling back over to them to get some of the hugs that were going around. Jina made space as Tony reached down to scoop him up for a group hug. As she kissed Robby's cheek, the doorbell rang.

Tony raised an eyebrow, wondering the same as Jina who would be coming over at that time, when a voice called in: "It's the Jameson's – anyone home?"

The Jameson's? Tony shifted Robby to his left arm and went to the door to open it.

"Hello, hey you guys! Chyna, Dean - "

"Hey," Chyna was the first to breeze in, her eyes wide. Jina stood watching the two as they entered, Dean just behind Chyna giving her a skeptical look. She knew what that meant.

"Oh wow, hello Tony!"

"Hi, Chyna, you two are here, together, wow. I forgot," Tony greeted them, looking a little dazed.

"We sure are," Chyna replied. "Seemed iffy for a minute there, I know, but yes, we got it together. I'll show you some pictures. You were at my wedding, Tone, and your wife is more than responsible for this union." She laughed. "Anyway, enough about that, how are you?"

"I'm doing good, thanks. Glad to be alive."

"I'll bet," Chyna exclaimed. "We saw the crash on the news and, oh my God, you look so great. Thank God you made it out of that wreckage." She moved forward to hug his neck and tickle Robby's chin. "We are just so relieved and I know Jina is too, though she probably hasn't said that, huh Sissy?" Chyna moved over to Jina where she also embraced her, towering over her as she did with everyone.

"I let him know how glad I was, and how glad I am, thank you," Jina said crisply. "Anyway, I thought you two were going to Africa?"

"Next week. We pushed it back a week to help Angie out with the kids, as Jojo is gone on a short-term project."

Jina nodded. For dramatic marriage stories, she couldn't touch her brother and his new bride: he'd had to leave not event days after their elopement. At the time, she didn't understand the rush, so may not have been as cordial to Angie and the kids as she could have.

She dismissed the thoughts: she would just have to think of something to welcome them. Jojo would not put up with any antics from her toward his new wife: whether she agreed or not, she was the last person to judge anyone.

"Um, how are they?" she asked. Dean gave her a look. "You can ask yourself by giving them a call."

Jina had no come back: he was right. "I'll do that," she said thoughtfully, challenging him to dare her. "Nice to see you too, little brother."

"Thanks." Dean planted a kiss on her cheek as she turned. "I thought you were getting a dog?"

"Don't. Be nice or leave," she warned.

"Dean's gonna be so nice, right Dean?" Chyna interrupted, looking daggers at him. "Jina's gonna be nice, too. And Robby is the sweetest, cutest thing I've ever seen!"

Dean looked back at Tony. Instead of saying anything after their curt initial greeting, Dean just nodded as he wordlessly took the child from Tony's arms.

"I'm always nice unless someone gives me cause not to be," he said evenly, before greeting Robby: "What up, little man?"

"There is no cause for anything, so cut it out," ordered

Chyna. "You know that Dean and Jina have a barking relationship. They try to see who can bark the loudest," she offered apologetically to Tony.

"I forgot that, but I'm seeing it, Chyna. Thanks for the Cliff notes. Are you the bark-o-meter, seeing which one has the worse bite?"

"Actually it's a bum game: neither is any worse than the other, isn't that right you two? They are both softies," Chyna whispered to Tony, loud enough for everyone to hear. "They do keep people guessing and on their toes, though. I've been around a long time, so I know their antics well."

Tony smiled, as did Jina. Even if Chyna Lockhart Jameson was a bit overly romantic - and being married to her knucklehead brother was proof of that; Jina would never understand quite how the two worked together - there was one thing that she did love about her longtime friend and eventual sister-in-law, and that was her cheery optimism. Everyone felt better with Chyna around. She'd been an integral part of their family since elementary school, when she'd first moved in just down the street from the Jameson family home. Later she'd become a rock for the entire family, caring for their ailing father until his death. She could never do any wrong in Jina's eyes. The whole family were that close: they trusted her with their lives. As far as Dean and Chyna were concerned, they'd taken forever to finally get their feelings in order long enough to marry. She was happy for them, but she didn't meddle, at least she tried not to meddle, in their affairs. She'd let Dean know soon enough that she'd appreciate the same courtesy from him as she endeavored to fix her own relationship.

She was glad her brother had found someone and all, but she drew the line at his badgering of her husband. Their relationship was strained enough. The fact that she grew angry at Dean, even if he was being a pest about their situation as usual, just showed how much she still loved Tony. She wouldn't take junk from anyone. Even if Dean felt he had a right to check in on where Tony's heart and head were at, now wasn't the time. She wasn't having it. They needed time to figure things out for themselves. She'd have a private talk with Dean later and would also let Tony know that she was not happy with her brother's way of doing things, even if it was supposedly in her honor. Chyna was good at refereeing, too. She was the no-nonsense type, always reminding each of them how important family was. The loss of her own parents and lack of biological siblings threw this into stark contrast.

Now, she looked around, her eyes widening. "You guys went on a shopping spree or what? Can we help you?"

"That sounds like a good idea," Tony chimed in, and Chyna smiled. "I can make us some dinner and we can chat some more," she suggested.

"Yeah, chat, that sounds good," Dean chimed in sarcastically.

"Dean," Jina warned. "If you're gonna stay, then-"

"He's gonna be on his best behavior, isn't that right honey?"

Dean rolled his eyes. "Maybe?"

Chyna gave him a sharp look. "He will. I promise."

"We can chat," Tony echoed firmly, to Jina's surprise. Dean's eyebrows raised at his agreement.

"Oh look, he came out of the accident nice and tough."

Jina crossed her arms defensively. "I'm warning you Dean, please." She knew how to get her way when she wanted - she wished that just sometimes her brother would heed her warnings.

She looked at the two of them, squaring off. Dean was overprotective: not more than Jojo – that would be impossible - but he was filling in for his brother nicely. She didn't appreciate him amping things up in Jojo's absence. They had enough to get through without Dean asking way too many questions that she and Tony had yet to discuss even between the two of them. She shot her brother one more stern warning look, and Dean finally seemed to back off.

"Ignore him," she told Tony, grabbing her child from Dean.

"I can handle it," Tony said, to her surprise. He nodded to her as she passed and for a moment, in his eyes, she saw the old him: the one that understood their silent communication perfectly. She turned, giving her brother another parting look for good measure, and marched into the living room. There, she tried to focus on Chyna and all her friend had to say, while pretending she wasn't listening intently to whatever went on in the kitchen between Tony and her brother.

12

"So, now that we're semi alone, Mr. you-can-handle-it, tell me: how in the hell did you get my sister back into the wiles of the devil?"

Tony bent to pick up a bag of groceries, placing them on the table. Dean's barbed question, albeit not how he would put it, was still a welcome one. If he was going to be with Jina, he had to take it all in – and, truth be told, he supposed he'd have the same kinds of questions if their roles were reversed.

"We were reconciling before my accident, if it's any consolation to you," Tony answered, after a pause, "but I obviously made a mistake in filing for divorce. I can't say I know what my reasons were exactly, but definitely not what I meant to do."

Dean hesitated, regarding the groceries. "You want some help in here?"

"Yeah, sure, thanks," replied Tony. "I know you probably have some questions for me."

"Some?" Dean said raising a brow.

"Okay, a lot of questions. I know. I can handle it, just as I said. I've always been a man of my word." Tony began to unpack some of the bags. Dean joined in, taking some stuff out and setting it on the table. Tony put the things away, still not having a clue what to make for dinner, but hurriedly eyeing the available items to make a decision. The faster he made dinner, the faster he and Dean could rejoin the women. He wanted to answer Dean truthfully and honestly, but that was hard to do with part of his memory MIA. However, he was fast working on a plan, and maybe some questions would help him clarify aspects of it. Search, find out the truth, then make amends to all the people he hurt, especially Jina. The more he was accused of, even, the more information he had to conduct follow-up research.

The small apartment was low on counter and cabinet space, but Tony made it work, looking at all that was before him as he put it away. Eventually he decided on a fettuccini with garlic butter, together with some bay scallops he'd just put into the freezer which he quickly retrieved, making sure there were enough for the four of them. He placed the items he would need on the small square of counter space by the stove.

"Chyna okay with scallops?" he asked Dean over his shoulder.

"Should be fine," Dean shrugged. "She likes your cooking."

"Okay, that's what I'll make." He tried not to wonder whether Dean had meant that he personally *didn't* like Tony's cooking, or if it was just another way of saying he was in some people's good graces but not everyone's.

"So first of all, do you know the damage that you caused?"

Tony stiffened. "I've seen some of it."

"What does that mean?"

"I've witnessed some of the ways I hurt Jina and my son."

"Really? Because sometimes I don't get that impression."

"You've been here all of five minutes," Tony defended.

"And you been here a week?"

It was less than that, actually, but he wouldn't give Dean the satisfaction. "That's not true, I was here before..."

"Before what?" Dean interrupted. "Before you jacked up your marriage, made my sister so crazy she'd give her own child to her sister to take care of? She was freaking giving up on everything. On her own child! Before you traded a perfectly good marriage for pleasing your father and that no-account sorry ass you call your best friend – oh, and your wicked step-Mommy."

Tony put down items he'd been putting away. This was the first time he'd heard that his father's wife played a role. She was a completely new person to consider. Other than being outright mean to Jina, he hadn't thought much about her at all in this mess. Dean's cutting looks and outright disdain hadn't been how he'd planned to gather information, but it was information he sought just the same.

"The more I think about and rack my brain for a plausible answer, the more I have come to realize there must be some kind of explanation," Tony reasoned.

"Sometimes there isn't any explanation," Dean snapped. "Sometimes people are just greedy: getting all they can get, doing the most, having a loving wife, a rich Daddy to buy them a nice car and house, even a side piece too, isn't enough."

"Look, I'm sorry. Whatever it was, whatever occurred, I'm sorry. My dad didn't..."

Now he was unsure. Had his father bought all of that? What about a salary? - what about being an actual employee and benefits for his wife? What the heck? Tony scrutinized everything Dean said, disbelieving. How did he even know? Is that what Jina had told him?

"I'm not divorcing Jina," he said. "I burned the papers."

Dean laughed, but his eyes were unwavering.

"She can still divorce you. I'm not so sure she shouldn't request copies of her own. Verdict still out on that one."

"Please don't - don't encourage her toward that," Tony pleaded.

"Why? Because she might just do it. She's not sure either. Time will tell."

"It will, and when it tells, I'll be with my wife and my family will be intact."

Just as casually as if they'd been talking about their respective golfing secrets, Dean washed his hands at the sink and fetched the plates, setting them on the table as Tony chopped up some parsley for the dish. The scallops swam in the butter and minced garlic. In the fresh silence, he added dry white wine and let it burn off before swirling the sauté pan around and around, turning off the heat under the cooked pasta. He drained it and started adding it to the plates, topping it with the scallops and sauce and grating fresh parmesan over each plate.

The dining room table was minimal but no one said anything as they all sat down.

"So what did you guys talk about?" Jina asked once they were all seated.

Tony shrugged but after the grace, he took a first bite, making sure everything tasted all right.

"This is so good," Chyna began. "Hey, I'm sure they discussed how Dean is going to recreate this sauce at home. I need a straw: it's just so good I want to drink it!" Everyone managed a laugh at that.

Dean nodded. "I was just telling my brother-in-law that there's two people in this relationship. You have to think about everyone, now Robby too, as you move forward."

"Ah yes, of course, no one can forget Robby," answered Chyna, gazing at the drowsy boy on her lap. "Of course Tony and Jina will do whatever is best for him. Who wouldn't do whatever they could for this cutie?" It was past his bedtime, but Tony didn't say anything as Chyna held him, seeming to enjoy keeping him close. Jina smiled and he tried to relax.

Tony managed a tight smile, thinking about some way to steer the conversation. He didn't want to pick a fight with Dean. He was listening. Whatever blame, whatever her family knew about the situation, whatever information they had or didn't have about the intimate aspects of their marriage didn't matter. He was working toward fixing it.

"I seem to recall an optometry office that burned down – was that your business, Dean? Did you decide what your second career was?"

"Yes, honey, what are you going to do when you return from Africa?" put in Chyna. "Because you can't hang around pestering me all day, and Tony is not letting you over here to pester him and Jina. So…"

"I'm probably going to teach at university," Dean responded. "We'll see. Verdict is still out."

"Yes, as protective as he is, I can just see him starting some kind of security detail," Chyna agreed.

"Well, stranger danger is all around."

"I can take care of myself, our threats are no more. There was a time yes, when the danger was real. You know Dean sent me away way back when; your sister, sneaky thing that she is, helped him - your mother too. They guilted me into leaving Dean at the worst possible time."

"Well, it worked, didn't it?"

"I'm not sure about that, you almost got yourself killed."

"It worked for a time," Dean clarified.

"Anyway…" Chyna rolled her eyes at Dean. Tony watched the two of them closely, recalling that at one time they'd had this love-hate relationship but had managed to get past it all to be together. He could barely remember the threat and the interworking of it all that Chyna now described. Dean's demeanor was obviously soft and kind toward his wife, despite his brash interrogation of Tony in the kitchen. Tony listened intently, to fill in the gaps of his own memory but also to see how Jina responded to hearing about it: to see if he could glean anything about what he and Jina had been doing at that time, or how their own marriage had been faring. Robby must have been an infant; he and Jina were together, and Lisa Stephens had been hanging around, causing trouble and wreaking havoc on Dean, before she'd moved on to him.

It was clear that the more Chyna spoke the tenser she grew, reliving everything that happened. She took a sip of her water and a big breath before setting her glass down.

"Our story of love, overcoming and moving past mistakes, miscommunications and deathly threats from outsiders, also suggests that you should never underestimate how far you'll go to protect the people you love - even to drive them away from you. I also lied then: to Warren, telling him I loved him, when there was absolutely no way I'd love anyone but Dean. It was a hard time, but we..."

"Got through it," Dean finished for her. "You can get through anything." Despite appearing to address Chyna, Dean looked pointedly at his sister, and that put Tony on edge. Their earlier discussion made him nervous about her ability to file for divorce, should it come that. It looked like Dean might even be encouraging her to leave her own husband – or maybe he was telling her that they could make it through together if they were willing. Sadly, Tony wasn't sure: he couldn't get a good read on the man.

Jina looked pointedly at Tony and he focused. Her smile gave him renewed hope. When she reached for his hand under the table, he gripped it like the life raft he needed. He dropped his fork and it clanked loudly on the edge of his plate. Everyone looked over, momentarily silent but otherwise without comment.

Lost in his own thoughts, he was aware that Dean was clearing the table and Chyna was helping. Whatever they said or did was a blur: he was lost in the last words Chyna had said.

"The scallops were cooked to perfection, how do you keep

them from getting so rubbery? And I'm not kidding, I want that sauce recipe so Dean can make it, soon," Chyna said, laughing. Tony smiled politely at her insistence. Tony assumed she didn't cook much herself and that Dean, like himself, made most of what the two ate. Before reaching for his plate, she handed a drowsy Robby back to him and Tony took him, cradling his head. He touched her hand. "I got this, you don't have to do that."

"I got it," she smiled. "I'm certain cooks don't clean up in the Jameson family. When you're a really good cook, you especially don't have to clean up."

Dean returned, collecting water glasses and silverware, before looking at Jina. "I brought you some new Rose and chocolate - you look tired, or I'd suggest we have a sip right now. We're gonna leave you two now, before you talk about us overstaying our welcome."

Jina stood and nodded. "Thanks. I am tired."

In less than twenty minutes, Dean and Chyna made quick work of dishes, doing what they could and managing to put everything away. Chyna and Jina had also been busy in the living room earlier in the evening: most of the floor was now visible once more.

When they were done, they grabbed their jackets and Jina met them at the door with Tony behind them.

"By the way, speaking of work as we were earlier, when are you going back to work for your Daddy?"

And Tony had thought the grilling was over. He looked down at his son, at Jina and Dean, all waiting expectantly for his answer.

"Sometime Monday maybe, but definitely next week," Tony answered honestly. It was always at the back of his mind. Next week seemed just as good a time as any to get his life going again.

"It was great to see you two," Chyna rushed out. "Listen, next week, uh - dinner at the family house, okay? Dean will make something delicious and I'll set a fabulous tablescape." Chyna laughed as she bent to embrace her friend. She kissed Robby on the forehead and touched Tony's arm before they left.

"You survived, you did great," Jina said, bringing Tony's head up in surprise.

"Are you encouraging me?"

She lifted a hand and let it slap against her thigh. "I'm trying."

"You're doing everything I don't deserve," he told her. Truthfully, he didn't think he gave her brother all the answers the man sought - but the fact was he didn't have all the answers. He only knew what he wanted and what he intended, and right now that had to work.

The two of them remained inside. Though she hadn't said anything about his revelation about returning to work, he turned to face her fully. "I'm gonna put him down and then we can talk. I know you have questions about what Dean and I discussed, and..."

"And what you just casually dropped oh, about ten seconds ago - there's that, too," Jina added.

"Yep, that too," he said. He kissed her quickly and scooted out of her grasp, knowing there was no way he was getting off the hook so easily. He did silently hope she passed out from exhaustion before they got to having it out about work. He wasn't sure that was going to be a point of contention, but even without the benefit of his memory, something told him he'd never be off the hook as far as Jina was concerned. What he'd found out today wasn't just about himself: he'd also discovered that Jina Jameson was more like her brother than she knew.

* * *

TONY EXITED the shower and resolved not to prolong the discussion he was about to have. He had given Robby the quickest bath the child had ever had and now he dried himself off quickly, even as thoughts traveled through his mind for what would likely be a tough discussion.

He mulled over what he could possibly say to override whatever issues Jina had about his return to work. He glanced at her as he donned an undershirt and shorts before crawling into his bed. He kissed her forehead and her eyes opened to look at him.

"Ready?"

"You purposely waited until I'm about to drop," she accused sleepily.

"I didn't!" Tony protested. "In fact, I went through a series of thoughts preparing for this, and I want to hear all you got to say."

Jina took a deep breath. "First, me first. I want you to know that I'm gonna try to be a big girl about this."

"Okay, great but before we get into that, at least tell me your fears."

Though she was hesitant, Jina let him pull her into his arms as he laid back against the headboard. "I want to hear the pros and cons and, most of all, I want to hear why you are afraid."

She hesitated. "There's a lot of them, ready?"

He nodded against her head, his chin resting on top of hers. She stretched out her fingers and ticked off the reasons one by one.

"One: that you'll get sucked back in by some kind of blind loyalty to your father. He's ill - you feel sorry for him – then that wife of his lays on some sort of guilt trip and lures you in with any number of reasons for your pity. Two: she'll spin a tale of your being in his will, and maybe you'll hold on thinking you have some sort of inheritance coming your way. It's the least your father can do, you might be thinking, for all the grief he gave you and your mother as a child, abandoning you all as he did. Three: you'll take his money to secure our future - and by that, I mean you'll suck it up and do the kind of work you hate day in and day out just because of Robby and I and our needs. Four: that there is a whole paid staff of folks who care so little for you that they haven't even had the courtesy to call and see how you are - more concerned about their jobs than they are about your wellbeing." She paused for breath. "I could go on."

"Here I thought you were sleepy," he said incredulously.

"I'm just out of fingers," she replied, looking back at him. "Basically, I'm imagining that it will be like my worst Groundhog Day. Over and over again, you being taken over with this work, then taken over with some kind of blind loyalty to your father - just taken, taken, taken away from me. I'm afraid that you'll lose sight of it all."

"But I have to know."

She nodded. "I know one person that will be more than happy for your return."

"Oh yeah, who is that?"

"Keith Munroe."

"We'll see," he said, uncertain.

She nodded, even as she yawned. "Listen." She pulled her head back and looked up at him. He leaned down to kiss her face again and again.

"Stop, you're distracting me."

"Your point is?"

She smiled. "I think there is one more thing, though."

"Okay, one more thing then lights out. What is it?"

"I think if this is what you want, it seems only logical to me that you won't just go into work blindly, but you'll…" She took a deep breath before rushing out her words: "Go see your father first."

13

hy was he even doing this?

Tony found himself at a set of brick columns that framed the iron gate of his father's estate. He felt the hairs standing up on the back of his head, and he didn't even have any hair. A chill washed over him as he turned onto the gravel road that led to his father's house. It was more like a compound, really: deep in the heart of Great Falls, Virginia, with big trees that hid the light of day and winding roads almost too bumpy for Jina's Lexus to handle. He could hear the rocks spit up and hit the car, so much that he slowed cautiously. Not a single light or sign pointed the way. If it had been night-time, he may not even have ventured further. How did anyone find the place? Just as Tony considered turning around, a small shelter seemed to appear in the middle of the road ahead. Armed guards waved him closer, where he stopped.

"Mr. King?"

No one called him that and he immediate thought of his father, but quickly spoke up lest they think he'd lost his mind – which, in some ways, he had.

"Yes, yes, hello. I'm here to see my father."

The guard regarded him coolly. "Is Mrs. King expecting you?"

"No, I didn't call, I just..."

The man nodded, disappearing abruptly inside the tinted booth. Tony heard a voice on the phone but couldn't make out what was said. When the man reemerged, he nodded him through. A guard on the other side lowered his gun and stepped aside as Tony inched forward before gradually picking up speed to pull away from the guard hut. It was another full mile before Tony reached the circular drive to park at the foot of the grand staircase that led to the front door.

He ascended the steps and, while he waited, turned to take in the view. He didn't know what he had been expecting, but while the house was large, it was old. The shrubbery was overgrown, and the steps so rickety that he had cautiously kept to one side of them as he climbed: the other side looked as if it might collapse under his weight. There was plenty of land, even a second house visible just to the north, and a pool – but it was full of fallen leaves, showing years of neglect and disrepair. He wasn't much of a landscaper, but even a novice could see that the entire place was in desperate need of attention. It would doubtless take some great length of time to rebuild.

The place made him feel sad with its eerily dilapidated state. Whatever he found out or didn't, he made up his mind right then that he didn't like how he felt, and he had no plans to visit again if he could help it. He thought about Jina momentarily, wondering if she had ever been here. He imagined she probably hadn't - and if she knew how bad it was, she likely wouldn't want to either.

A woman finally appeared at the door. Tony remembered her from the hospital, but otherwise didn't feel anything toward her.

"It's so good to see you. I thought you'd never come," the strange woman said breathlessly. Her eyes glued to his, she leaned closer, scrutinizing and smiling.

Catching him off guard, the woman yanked Tony's hand, pulling him inside and closing the door at his back. She hugged him and stood back.

"How are you? I wanted to call and see how you were doing. I visited the house but I didn't see you there… so you must have been staying with Jina?"

Tony raised his eyebrows in confusion. "She's my wife - why wouldn't I have been staying with her?"

"Of course, of course, for a little while I guess, until…" The woman trailed off.

"Until what?" he questioned, not liking what she implied nor knowing quite what she meant. "I just wanted to see my father."

She continued to stare at him expectantly. Something about her made him uncomfortable and he resolved to check on his father and leave as quickly as possible.

"Of course, of course." The woman nodded but she looked at him from under her long lashes, smiling in an oddly coy fashion. "Look, I know you're always so formal, but there's no one here… just so you know, you don't have to pretend."

"Pretend what? I'm not pretending." He didn't know what she meant. "No one here like… who?"

"I just mean that we have staff, a chef, of course, but they're gone for the day. I let most of the staff go since your father had taken a turn for the worse."

"He has?"

"Yes, even before your uh, accident."

Tony nodded. Searching for somewhere to look besides at her, he took in the house. A large space, the place seemed as if at one point it time it might have been quite grand. Now, however, it was eerily quiet: almost cave-like. The three chandeliers above were dimmed, and the space was devoid of any real décor, save a table with a large granite vase holding tall artificial flowers – and an inch of dust. Her voice echoed, bouncing all around the walls with no soft furnishings to absorb it. The sound was hollow and loud, despite it being just the two of them in the mansion. It was unusually dark, he also noticed. The curtains were drawn everywhere he looked, permitting no one to see out and certainly not letting in any light.

"Down this way," she said over her shoulder, as she led him toward a room way in the back of the house. A series of lamps illuminated the otherwise dim room: a small desk and, to his surprise, a lone figure lying in a stark white hospital bed.

Tony stood, rooted to the spot, and just stared. Whatever he'd expected, he never once thought he'd see his father in such a state. While there wasn't a ton of machinery, the tube from a single oxygen tank wound its way up to a cannula under his father's nostrils. It made the only sound in the room. On the bedside table stood a pitcher of water and numerous medication bottles of varying sizes, each full of pills lined up like tiny soldiers waiting to be deployed. He wondered momentarily whether the man before him was even his father. The figure lay unmoving, his tan face wrinkled and pale, seeming almost colorless.

"What - uh, what is he dying of?"

"He has cancer. It's been devastating and hard."

"What?" Tony couldn't believe any of that. "Where, where is his doctor?"

"He was here, uh, earlier this week," she rushed out. "He only comes about once a week now, but I have him on call. He – uh, says there's not much to do, except to make him comfortable."

Tony moved closer and looked down, finally feeling as if he had some composure. Although he didn't care for his father after those years of abandonment, all that suddenly seemed terribly trivial, sailing out the window the moment he entered the room to see the defenseless man lying there so still, probably not even knowing he was there. All at once

Tony felt sorry. Despite everything, he wasn't incapable of caring.

He reached for his father's hand but stopped when she touched his arm.

"Please don't - please don't disturb him?"

"I just wanted to..."

She cut him off. "I know, I know, but every time he wakes up, he's excitable." She sighed. "It's like he's fighting the inevitable."

"What does that mean?"

"Oh honey, don't look at me like that. He's dying. He's dying, okay? Isn't it plain to see?"

For a moment, he thought she was hysterical, but she quickly calmed and turned away from him, collecting herself. She turned back, smiling and brushing away the tears that had entered her eyes.

"I'm sorry," Tony offered, nonplussed. "I'm sorry, I just didn't expect..."

"I know, I see it every day and it's still a shock."

"I'm sure." He nodded. Though he wanted on one hand to exhibit concern for her and this entirely tragic situation, the other part of him was reminded of the way in which she had treated Jina in the hospital. He was cautious of her motives. All the little allusions without outright saying what she meant, all the convoluted hedging, as if somehow trying to get him to admit or say something he didn't mean, was not sitting right with him. Not to mention that she'd seemed to imply he shouldn't be with his wife, as if it was over, when that wasn't what he wanted things to be at all.

He couldn't reconcile the woman in the hospital and the woman before him, so he didn't bother. Jina's words about the woman before him replaying in his head.

He was startled when his father's eyes opened abruptly, lifting, staring, before coming to rest on him. The older man made a sudden move, grabbing the hand that rested on his left by the bed and gripping it surprisingly hard, startling Tony. He made a noise, but Tony, shocked that he moved at all, didn't know what he was trying to say. Somehow, his father's eyes felt as if they were pleading with him.

"TTTTeeee,eeee - "

Tony tried to make it out, tried to say something that would calm his father down.

"I'm here, I'm here," he murmured. "What's the matter?" Tony looked around and saw the woman over at the small dresser fumbling with some bottles, evidently having not noticed what was happening. He turned back to face his father.

"Dad." His voice and the label he used came awkwardly to his lips, sounding foreign to him. "Dad, please, rest, stop." The strength of his father's grip almost hurt his hand, but something in him wouldn't let him shrug him off.

When she approached, his father grew more agitated and Tony noticed he was almost crying, recoiling from her. His father almost screamed at that point, and the sound brought Tony a feeling he couldn't say he'd ever had before.

"Stop, stop, what are you doing?" he exclaimed. His father still gripping him, Tony watched her as she inserted a needle into a clear glass bottle and slid it out before moving closer to his father on the other side of the bed. Before Tony could think of what to do, she took his father's arm forcefully. He tried to shrug away, and when she injected him, she took a deep breath, squeezing her eyes tight.

His father's sounds stopped and where he'd been holding Tony's hand so tightly, now the hand loosed him altogether, falling limply back onto the bed.

"Look I'm sorry - I'm sorry you had to see that," she said, panting a little. "It's just a pain killer, it relaxes him and it makes him feel good. Okay? It's okay. I've been trained to do this - I've been doing it for a few weeks now. His frantic fits, they're, they're getting worse."

She seemed unhinged, Tony thought, and yet his own trauma about whatever had just happened felt amped up. Blood surged through his veins and his heart beat wildly. He stepped back. She, in contrast, was no-nonsense again, as if nothing at all had transpired: completely unaffected by his father's frantic cries of pain and her recent ministrations. She didn't say any more about anything, just continued moving about the room wordlessly, fixing things up, closing bottles, putting the needle into a type of red box he'd only seen in a hospital setting.

He was forced to back away from the bed when she moved to clean his father's mouth and brush his brow with a damp cloth, taking Tony's place as she tucked the covers around him as perfectly as if she was making up a bed at the Ritz: as if nothing had happened at all.

"Please let's let him rest," she said almost angrily, seeming suddenly to admonish him.

Tony exited the room wordlessly to the hall and stood, unsure of what to do next.

The loud bang of the doors closing caused him to look over. "Honey, I am trying to be patient, but how long am I supposed to wait?"

Tony crossed his arms over his chest and stared at her blankly. "Wait for what?"

"Wait, wait, for your father to, to...die?" she said it as if there wasn't anything else to be said. "Don't give me that look. I have been here caring for him for almost a year. Everyone else has been run off by his tantrums."

"Is that what you call what just happened?

"No, no, of course not, but that's what we revert back to, isn't it? Childlike behavior. I'm saying care is so very hard to find, it's rather impossible... and then your accident and you, you working at the company all the time..."

He didn't follow her at all. "What am I supposed to do?"

"See me!" she exclaimed. "Even though I know you're in

the middle of wrapping things up with Jina, you could at least visit. You're over there playing house with your ex-wife, what on earth am I supposed to think?" She threw up her hands in apparent exasperation.

"What are you even talking about?" Tony felt exhausted and he hadn't even been there a full hour. He also felt angry that she thought he was pretending. *Why?*

"Us! I'm talking about us and the life we're supposed to be building together here?"

"What is that supposed to mean? My life is with my wife, I'm not divorcing her." Tony was confounded.

"What do you mean you're not divorcing her? How will you secure our future, how will you take over the company? Your father is doing worse and worse. It's time to get this show on the road!"

"What show are you talking about?"

"Is your memory back or what?"

"No, not completely…" A part of him wanted to lie and tell her it had returned; but perhaps she assumed he had part of it and that's why she'd divulged as much as she did. What was odd, he reflected, was that everyone worried whether it was a good idea to give him details about his past - whether they should or shouldn't. Tisha and Chase had been similarly concerned about divulging too much owing to their care for him. That couldn't be said for Sheila King. She wanted him to remember, and quickly, because whatever the information was could somehow benefit her. That's what he sensed, although of course he couldn't be sure. Was she the one that he hadn't named? *Had he cheated on his wife with his father's wife?* He was disgusted by the thought, trying not to believe it even as he wondered.

"But, but," she stuttered, "why did you come over here? You must remember *something*?"

"It was Jina's idea that I come to check on my father, see how he was doing," Tony faltered. His heart rate increased as new revelations came to him, too quickly to catalog and far too upsetting to accept as the real truth. He had more than enough information on how his father was 'doing'. None of it was good. The rest of his plans for the day were quickly sailing out the window: going to work versus getting back home to Jina, where things made more sense, were rapidly switching places on his list. He longed for her calm, even as he told himself he didn't deserve her at all. If all this was true, he really didn't deserve her: he was an awful person and Dean had every right to have such disdain for him as he did. If all this was true, he finally understood everyone's wariness.

"After I stopped by here to see my father, I was planning to head to the office, to see how things are there. I... didn't know he was like that," he continued, even though his mind was reworking his schedule. Considering the last hour's events, he was almost scared about what he might find at his so-called job. Was this something that just might have to wait another day, or a week, or never? He would quit before he would believe whatever she said was true. It wouldn't be that hard, considering he couldn't remember what on earth possessed him to take up professionally with his father in the first place.

Now, all he knew was that he was ready to go.

He moved toward the door. "This plan that you insist we have, why don't you just tell me the details? Why don't you start from the beginning? Tell me exactly what you are talking about."

Suddenly, her entire demeanor changed, her anger growing. "I am *talking* about your leaving your wife and us building our lives!" Her hands balled into fists and she leaned in, right in his face. "As odd as this seems, we - by that I mean you and me - fell in love," she said, more softly. "You would never hurt your father, of course, but that was the promise you made to me. You being with Jina isn't the plan, I tried to tell you that in the hospital. I tried to tell her, too, but you stopped me from saying a single word to her. Then she left so abruptly, never wanting to hear the truth. I realize that she is so fragile that she can't possibly handle you falling out of love with her, but you had a plan. You didn't tell me how you were going to get out of your marriage, but you did promise you would. In fact, I thought you had: you served her the divorce papers, and you said you would figure it out. Stupid me, I believed you. I believed you and now the accident, I thought I'd lost you!"

She rushed to him and her hands moved up his chest. "This isn't the plan we had, Tony! Your father is dying; you are supposed to take over and fix the company in his absence. Now, when you are appointed CEO, we are going to get married and have our baby. I've been waiting for you. *We've* been waiting for you. Please tell me you remember - I mean, that's why you're here, right? You remember? You don't have to act like you care about your father, hon - there's no one here but us, I mean, apart from him, of course," she laughed. "As you can see, he's in no shape to do anything."

Tony could barely bring himself to look away. He was shocked into silence, his world crumbling with the new knowledge of the pain he had caused and no off-ramp in sight. He had no idea what to do or how to respond.

"Oh Tony," she said with tears in her eyes. "I'm - we're - " She rubbed her protruding belly. "Look, we didn't... you have not told Jina because she was having some issues okay? Her mind is not all there, she's just not been handling your separation well, and - " The woman twirled a glittery tipped index finger against her temple and rolled her eyes, smirking. "Cray-cray, babe. She couldn't handle this." She spread her hands wide. "You can't tell her that I'm carrying your child, okay? But it's the truth," she whispered as a tear snaked down her face. "And *that* is the plan I'm speaking of. Now, please tell me, tell me you remember this, Tony - please?"

14

You're lying. Those were the last words he said to her, even as his body filled with anger at her statements. They couldn't be true. They just couldn't. Tony had calmly exited the event even as she tried to hold him there, pleading. He remembered her hands grabbing him, pulling at him to stay. He didn't want to hurt her, considering her condition, but he was not going to stay there and continue to listen. He wasn't sure, but he believed in his gut she was lying. There was no way this is what he'd been planning.

His car was back on the I-95 before he even knew where he was going. He eased his foot off the gas lest he crash again. From his rearview mirror he saw nothing but cars, but in his mind's eye he saw her: his father's wife, or whatever she was. Tony took a deep breath, focusing on calming himself down. He heard the phone ring in his pocket and he pulled over. He needed a moment anyway.

"Hey listen man, it's been about a week or so. I was, uh, hoping I could talk you into coming back to work today? I have some important meetings, and I need you to meet with some folks."

Tony knew it was Keith Munroe, it said as much on his

caller ID; but he found it odd to be hearing from him on the very day he'd decided to go back to work.

"I have some questions about our business, Keith." Tony wasn't ready for much of the day but he would go for at least a few hours.

"Sure man, I can give you all the details. I'm surprised you're agreeable to coming by, though - I thought you'd be taking a little more time to recover?"

"Yeah, no. I'm ready to get my life back together, see what's what," Tony answered. *Boy, was that the truth.*

"Oh man, I'm glad to hear that. Literally the best news I've heard all month."

"Yeah?"

"Yeah, man. I thought you'd be wrapped up in that wife of yours," came Keith's reply. "I mean, she hates your work, ya know, but it's good for a man to have something to do with his time, know what I mean? Work is good -dignifying. Uh, when can I expect you bruh?"

Tony quickly looked for an address. One thing he was certain he had to do was to stop letting everyone tell him the way things were and figure out some of this mess for himself, and from there on out stop taking everyone's word as the truth. People lied. Before he met Jina and her family, he believed that strongly for some reason. Her family taught him a lot about being in a family. Up until meeting Jina and the rest of them, he had trusted no one but himself. Barring her and the rest of the Jamesons, he felt himself being drawn back into that way of thinking. Being skeptical and suspicious kept him intact: there was nothing wrong with a healthy dose of optimism, but somewhere along the line he'd obviously trusted the wrong people and lost sight of the things that were important to him. No more. It was clear there were those he could trust and those he needed to reserve judgment on until he had the right information.

He opened the web browser and did a quick search of his father's name. Two locations popped up.

"The DC HQ, is that the primary?" he asked.

"Yeah, man you're on it."

Tony nodded. He put the address into the GPS and gave Keith his estimated time of arrival.

"All righty then, see ya in a hot minute."

"Yep."

Tony put the phone down on the seat beside him and, speeding back up to the flow of traffic, he eased back into the proper lane, heading off to see what exactly he'd gotten himself into. He had a renewed urgency to put his life back in the proper order, with Jina, and get to the truth. What Sheila King was saying just couldn't be it.

* * *

KEITH PRESSED a button on the desk phone: "Clean this place up, Mr. King is on his way."

He swiveled back and forth in his chair, taking in the view he'd had for almost three wonderfully unbothered weeks, and sulked: he'd have to give it up – only temporarily, but give it up just the same. Having another thought, he dialed a second number.

"Sorry, had to give him a call. I should have waited, but if he was as angry as you say when he left, it seemed like a good time to pile on. You surprise me, woman - I can't believe you told him everything." Keith laughed bitterly. "He seems determined, a little glimpse of his old self. He's definitely feeling a little gruff, but maybe he's remembering some things, maybe not. Hard to tell. Either way, he seemed eager to get to work."

He listened for a beat. "Of course, I'll get the board to appoint him. We're just being tested, got to be a little patient. How is the old man? Still hanging on? I thought you upped the dosage?... Oh yeah, don't want to give him too much.

Gotta look like an accident. Right. You gave up nursing for this caregiver gig, and now I'd say you're almost set for life."

He paused and smiled. "Of course I'll hold up my end of the bargain. Let me get back to my stupid cubicle. Now that he's back, gotta resume my life as a gopher... Yeah, I'll keep you posted, but keep insisting. Threaten he wife if you have to. If he's really Team Jina, you'll find out by threatening her. K. Later."

Keith picked up the item he'd been working on just as the office cleaners rolled in the loud trashcan. Keith stood, holding the papers close to his vest, eying them warily.

"Mr. Munrow."

Keith's eyes darkened, thinking of all his plans.

"Sir? Sorry, yes sir."

His eyes cut them. "Get this place cleaned up," he snapped. "You have less than an hour. Hurry up." Leaving the large office, he returned to his own small cubicle. It helped to know he would only be in that hole for another couple of months. It couldn't be helped: the goal had moved only slightly, but it wasn't out of sight. He'd be CEO by January 1 and Tony would be dead, again, because he'd obviously refused to die the first time.

* * *

JINA PICKED up the phone after swigging a mouthful of water. Surprised to see Tony calling, she quickly slid the button that put him through.

"Hi" she said, glad to hear his voice after a full day. Despite having initially felt so weird with him around all the time, it did feel lonely with him gone, even if it was only for a few hours so far. Her heart sped: it was like old times, where he'd call in the middle of the day just to check on her and see how she and Robby were doing. She missed those calls.

"Hey, I thought I'd just give you a call."

She tried not to sound overly elated. "That's nice, are you doing OK? How's your dad?"

She knew from the silence that it might not have been good. She waited patiently for him to speak.

"It's ah, a little bit worse than I thought."

"Oh, I'm - I'm sorry to hear that."

"Yeah, me too. I'm just gonna spend a few hours here at the office for my first day, try to ease myself back into a schedule – but, Jina, I am going to make a promise to you right now that I am going to do everything I can to be home every single night to eat dinner and to be present because I love you so much."

She hadn't expected the urgency in his voice. She sat up straighter, with the strange feeling that something was horribly wrong. Maybe his father was much worse than she imagined, or even than he was letting on. His "Okay," however it came, it was still welcome to hear. She leaned her head into the phone, as silly as it felt, just wanting to be close to him. "I -I love you too," she replied. "I can't wait to see you. Robby and I actually went for a walk today. I did some blogging, and Robby has a play date tomorrow. I'm kind of looking forward to it. Oh, and I talked to Angie. I was thinking her and the kids could come over and we could have some dinner. I'm going to try to not look at her in such a bad light, despite my brother's harebrained idea of marrying her right before going off on tour. But anyway, I'll tell you more about that later. I'm just… let's just say I'm gonna get it together and be the best auntie I can be for them."

"I'm sure you can do it."

She laughed but appreciated his encouragement. She wondered just how much he remembered about her other brother, Jojo, and his new wife. They'd eloped, then off on his next tour of duty he went. She'd seem him only briefly after Tony's accident, then he was off to war-torn worlds unknown. She said a quick prayer for him and for Tony too: that his day would improve and his father, whatever was going on with him, would transition peacefully.

"That sounds good," came Tony's voice. "I'm gonna have to go but Jina, I just... I love you so much. I never want you to doubt that, not for a single moment."

"OK, baby, that sounds ominous, but rest assured I like hearing it," she laughed nervously.

"Well get used to it, because I'm'a tell you every day for the rest of your life if I have to; sometimes two or three times a day. I won't need a reminder ever again."

"Okay, Tony. Just be careful out there, please. And I wanted you to know that, uh - "

"Tell me"

"I was just thinking about what I will do after this baby is born. I thought I'd go back to work, but maybe I can work remotely, to stay with them more, or even do something part time. I just don't want you to feel a sense of blind loyalty to your father, okay? You're not the reason he's sick. You're trying to do right by him and his affairs."

She heard silence on the phone, but the background street noise told her he was still on the line. She felt sad knowing all the years he and his father had lost, and sensing that taking on the business was Tony's way to try to make it right, doing whatever he could with what was left. Regardless of what Tony felt and what it had done to their marriage, this current state of affairs wasn't entirely his fault. She had some blind ambitions too once upon a time, and it had taken losing her marriage and several miscarriages to finally bring her clarity. Every person had to arrive at their own conclusions, she believed, and that also meant on their own timeline. She realized that now: whatever he was trying to do for his father, his heart had initially been in the right place and that was what mattered. Each time she felt resentment in some form, she had to come back to his intention.

"I'm clued in, baby. Jina, don't you ever give me a pass. I don't deserve it. I don't deserve you."

Jina smiled. She was a little concerned about the tone of his voice, but she chalked it up to the heightened emotion from seeing his father. Whatever state he was in couldn't have been encouraging. She thought back to her own father's diagnosis and what had seemed like a painfully slow decline. She wanted to ask Tony more, but she knew he had to go. This wasn't the time for her to share all she knew about his father's business and the man he used to be, or to relive her own father's health journey to his eventual death. One thing Tony might want to know that she would be sure to tell him is that his father hadn't given interviews or even been seen publicly in the last two years. That alone said a lot. She'd also see if he wanted to see some videos showing his father, or if that might be too painful: to give him a glimpse of the shrewd businessman his father once was.

They said their goodbyes. He was feeling extra sappy and however it came about, she'd take it. His over-the-top statements of love made her happy.

"See ya tonight," she offered, not wanting to keep him from finishing the day's business and getting home to her and their son.

"Tonight, before dark," he assured her, and then the line was silent.

Feeling a slight uptick in energy for the first time in a while, Jina got out her laptop. She wiped the thin sheen of dust from the metal case then slapped her leg, leaving a grey handprint on her dark leggings as she logged in and immediately started frantically clicking through a series of websites to get some information about Tony's father. She bookmarked a couple sites, also copying a number of relevant URL's into her notes. Hearing Robby cry, she scrolled through the headlines more quickly. Her fingers seemed to itch with the need to research something. When Robby fussed again, she stood up, bookmarking one last website before setting the computer aside and heading for Robby's room. Maybe this would just be something for Tony to focus on.

The question of whether she could really help him lingered in her mind. Thoughts of doing anything of an investigative nature stirred her: it was like she'd felt when assigned to a hot story, on a trail of evidence, with new questions and new ideas.

She laughed and gave herself a little shake: she'd just been looking up old news, don't get carried away. What is the story here anyway? An old man is dying, his weirdo-too-young wife would inherit a fortune and get herself another old man to swindle, leaving the poor baby she carried to fend for himself or be raised by an overpaid au pair. Despite her own feelings about carrying another child, she tried not to resent Sheila King for getting pregnant in a matter of months after marrying the man, doing so only to secure her future, one suspected. "Lord forgive me," she uttered, hating to jump to the conclusion that the child wouldn't be loved when she had no basis for that supposition barring her dislike for the woman. Regardless, Jina hated to see how Sheila seemed to rope so many into her snares, including a lonely old man.

"Sometimes, Robby honey, there isn't anything to the story and we must quell our imaginations, baby," she murmured. "Stop making up junk where there isn't any." She let Robby lead her out of the room and to the kitchen, where she would make them both a snack. Despite putting her newshound nose to the side, she was surprised by how even just a few minutes of looking up websites, undertaking research and clicking through those clackety computer keys had seemed to invigorate her, for the first time in a very long time. "And sometimes," she added mysteriously, looking down at her son, "it's even worse than you think." She laughed at her son, who clapped his hands jovially back at her.

15

To say Tony was mentally exhausted when he got home was a major understatement. He stood just inside the kitchen, staring blankly but so glad to be back in his own home.

Mindlessly, he turned to wash his hands at the sink. Though he hadn't been expecting it, he breathed a sigh of relief as arms came up around his waist. Grabbing a dish towel and drying his hands, he slowly turned in Jina's arms and hugged her close. His hands were full of her amber knit top. She felt amazing against him, soft, warm, and familiar, inviting in a way that she hadn't often been in the last few weeks. It was a welcome surprise of affection from her.

"So how was it?" he heard Jina mumble against his chest. He looked down at her as she turned her face toward his. He couldn't help but close the distance between their mouths, bending to fuse his lips against hers, stealing kisses like a man sinking on the coast.

She giggled when he let up. "That bad or that good?"

"Verdict still out," Tony replied. "Mostly bad, though. It's definitely nothing great." They walked to the dining area where Tony loosened his shirt and sat down, looking at her.

He was surprised to see the table set, a glass of wine for him, water for her, and dishes, but no food and no smells of anything cooking in the oven.

"I took the liberty of ordering something I hope you'll like," she said coyly. "You've had it before, but I didn't want you to cook and I wasn't going to top off your day with another disaster, so I..." - she stopped midsentence as the doorbell rang and moved to the doorway - "ordered out."

He heard some talking, then the door closed and she returned with a brown paper sack.

"It's not Chinese, just this little hole in the wall down the street."

Tony nodded as she pulled thick foiled containers from the bag. Until the smells wafted passed his nose, he hadn't thought about being hungry much at all. The thick sandwich he unwrapped before him changed all of that, however, and after saying grace holding her hand, he dug in with a huge first bite. "Oh wow – that's good."

She smiled, digging into her own sandwich. "Well now, I may not cook much but I can order the best of the best *from* the best and get it right here to our door." Tony wiped his mouth, savoring the juicy bits of steak, the tangy sauce and the gooey cheese. He was impressed: it was rich, juicy and thick. He fed her a fry and she squished one, blowing on it before sharing it with Robby, who drooled in delight gnawing at his mother's offering.

Whatever Keith had said seemed awfully evasive. Keith had been of no help as Tony had tried to find out what kind of business his father operated: he talked fast, he moved fast, his entire being was flashy and that annoyed Tony, who felt that he couldn't get a real read on the man. The more he listened, the more this whole operation seemed like a farce.

Tony looked at her as he dug into his sandwich. He couldn't help but be intrigued by the image of his father, upright, suit-wearing, articulate and lucid. It was a stark contrast to what he had seen just earlier that day.

"Listen to me, I don't know if this is a good idea, so I'm concerned that this might just make you – oh, I don't know..."

"What?"

She looked at him. "More depressed."

Tony nodded, understanding the reason for her hesitation. She was so right. She thought ahead: of how much he could handle. Part of him wanted desperately to tell her about all the things that Sheila had said, but he couldn't - not yet. He couldn't believe he'd done that: not *that*. Anything but that.

"Watching videos of my father, the few we have... well, sometimes you have to be in the right head space for it all, and it often isn't of any comfort to me, but Dean and Tish seem to like looking at him years ago," Jina explained. "As for Jojo and I, we can't look without the pain. Nothing is as good as the memories, however good the picture is, however clear the audio, it's not the same. The memories you have trump the images of everything - and I love my father. I have to think that somewhere deep down inside, you do have love for yours, too."

Tony hesitated. "It was strange today," he reflected after a moment. "I just felt sad. I felt like I missed out. I mean, I've had resentment, all of that. But I wouldn't wish him any illness, regardless."

Tony put the computer to the side thoughtfully, wondering why in the world he would ever risk his entire family and, on a related note, would he want to see that version of his father? How would it make him feel?

"I do want to see any videos you have," he told her at last. "Thank you for thinking about this." He leaned in to kiss her. "I'll take a look tonight before bed. Thank you."

They ate the rest of their food in silence. Tony tried to remain present, knowing that later that night he'd be glued to the screen finding out everything there was to know about his father, working hard to uncover whatever could fill in the blanks in his memory.

* * *

DESPITE GOING through all the motions for what had become their easy night routine, the computer and the videos lingered on his mind. He'd managed to give Robby a bath, spent some time reading to him and cleaned up after their dinner. He patted his stomach, knowing he needed to get back to the gym and his normal workout regimen.

When the water stopped, he heard Jina exit the bathroom. She sat on the bed and looked at him, wrapped in nothing but a towel. The suggestion in her eyes told him a lot.

Jina sighed. "I wanted tonight to be kind of special, but this baby stuff is no joke on the fatigue front."

Tony raised an eyebrow. "Oh really?" he grinned.

"That's the point," she said with a sad smile. "I was raring to go… but now I'm just tired."

"That is completely fine." A part of him was glad: sadly enough, almost relieved. He wanted her and that desire to know his wife again hadn't left him. The truth was, though, that he didn't have all the facts, and right now that hung over him like a dark cloud. A part of him knew he should tell her what he'd learned, but first he had to be sure of the truth.

"I'm gonna fall asleep on you, that would be no fun," she continued. "I want to participate."

He couldn't help but smile. "Listen, my randy little pregnant wife, we got all the time in the world."

"Do we?"

The seriousness of her question caused him to stare at her, hating that she had a single doubt about the two of them and hating too that he had caused that doubt, yet she still offered herself to him. She loved him. There wasn't any other explanation. She knew the truth; he'd hurt her, maybe even threatened her about...

"Yes, he assured her.

Jina bridled at the pause before his response. "Did you hesitate?"

"No. No, I just hate that what I did caused you to doubt. That pains me."

"Look at me. I said that I forgave you and I do. My dreams - "

"Which you have not had since we've been home," he reminded her.

"Yes," she conceded. "I noticed, Tony, I have always felt safe when you've been here. I haven't ever felt afraid knowing you're here and that Robby's with Tish. When I first moved in here, I was scared one night, not having lived alone for a very long time. Then you came over. You knew I was scared and you ended up staying."

"That's how it happened. Interesting. Perhaps you lured me here under the guise of your fear," he teased.

"I wouldn't do that. I don't play games," she said firmly.

"I know it - that was a joke." *A poor one*, he admonished himself. "Listen, back to our original discussion: anytime, anyplace, you name it, and when our energies match, it's on, make no mistake. I can't wait. You got it." He moved down in the bed, drawing her close. He helped her towel dry and located the shirt she'd put out at the end of the bed, helping her into it. Despite the modest way she held the towel to cover up, he caught a brief glimpse of her stomach and saw it starting to protrude slightly with the child they'd made together growing inside.

When she laid back, he pulled her close as he opened the laptop. Jina leaned against his chest; he felt her body relax and knew she drifted, even as he quietly clicked a series of links she'd emailed him and read the articles. Jina snuggled closer, but after only a few minutes she sat up with a start.

"Oh my God, Tony?"

He put the computer away momentarily concerned. "What is it?"

"I can't believe I forgot but I have baby brain. I didn't ask you how Miss Vera was doing when you went over there today? You didn't mention her, and you know she's crazy about you. How is she doing?"

Tony's eyebrows rose. He was glad there was no emergency, but he was confused. Other than the guards, his father and his father's wife, he hadn't encountered a single person that day. Sheila had mentioned a chef but hadn't indicated there was anyone else there.

"Uh, Vera? I don't know who that is," he admitted.

"You're kidding, Tony? Oh my God, you're serious. She used to work for your father: she seemed like she really tried to take care of him, despite that horrible woman. If your stepmother's nastiness ran her off, you should be concerned. She was your father's only ally." She turned to Tony. "I mean, that can't be good for your father - he needs an advocate. Ms. Vera had been there for almost six years: before he took ill, before you and your father met again, even. Oh Tony, if Ms. Vera was fired, can you at least check to see if she got a severance package or something? I'll look for her address tomorrow. I'm sure I have it."

Tony thought. "The odd thing is that she – Sheila, I mean – did comment that she couldn't keep caregivers on because of his - she called them tantrums, which kind of made me mad."

"What?" Jina was incredulous. "Man, she is something. It would make you mad. *I'm* mad! How dare she say that? He's not a child."

"Well, she seemed to think old people just revert back to being child-like as they get older. She said that before she gave him a dose of whatever she gave him it was terrible."

"And a nurse should be doing that," Jina put in. "Is she a freakin' nurse among her many other talents?"

"Shesaid she'd learned how - was trained, or something," Tony clarified.

"Oh boy." Jina rubbed her temples, the distress she showed over what he shared only serving to increase Tony's own concern.

"Okay fine. Just please get in touch with Ms. Vera, honey. Make sure that she got a proper compensation of some sort for her service to your dad. It wasn't that long a time, but she was older, she deserved some kind of package?"

"Of course, of course I want to talk to her. She may even have some info on Dad's condition before he got worse. I was also planning to try to get in touch with one of his doctors and see what else I can find." He didn't add that his father, and now Sheila, had money and access to some of the best specialists around: saying as much might cause Jina more alarm than he wanted to just then.

"J, of course, I definitely want to talk to her; thank you for remembering her. I should find her, but Jina? I want you to stay away from this situation, however things pan out."

"Okay," she agreed reluctantly. "You do think everything is all right, don't you?"

He nodded. "Yes, but I just… won't give her any opportunity to contact you. Ever. Just stay away from her." Jina seemed to agree, and Tony was relieved. He leaned back, opening his right arm to her, and she willingly settled against him once again and fell asleep in mere moments. "Don't shay up all night looking at that, oshay?" she mumbled sleepily. He smiled down at her drowsy eyelids fighting the fatigue that came with her pregnancy. He loved her. His heart beat wildly at the very thought of losing her and his son. For what? He wasn't that man. He wasn't.

To ensure she didn't hurt her neck or back, Tony gently helped her lay her back on her own pillow. "Goodnight." He kissed her, promising to do as she asked, before pulling the covers up around her. He dimmed the laptop screen and searched his nightstand for a pair of ear buds, plugging only one bud into his left ear. If Robby called out, he wanted to be able to hear. He pulled up a video and hit play. Everything his father had been flashed before his eyes, from his serious and strong voice to his pristine double-breasted suit. Tony watched, amazed. He never recalled any of these things about his father.

On the screen before him, Tony clicked the play button, and watched closely as a man nearing death came to life.

16

Tony didn't want to waste any more time. In the course of a single night, he'd listened to almost ten hours of video of his father - and found a man he really didn't know. His father, he discovered, was a savvy businessman, a real estate mogul, a philanthropist even; but, frankly, he sucked at relationships. There were lots of women to go along with almost every story Tony had watched, one even claiming an illegitimate child that he'd supposedly fathered.

According to Jina's wishes, he located Ms. Vera in a matter of days, stood now at her house's front door, at a reasonable hour that morning. The broken-down home that in the neighborhood of mostly neat brick ramblers, looked conspicuously the worse for wear.

He pushed the doorbell and heard dogs barking in the back. When no one came after several minutes, he decided to go around to the back, where the barking grew louder.

"Who is there? Hush now, you two. Oh hello, can I help you?" came a frail voice.

"Hello - Ms. Vera?

"Oh my God, lil Tony?"

Tony moved closer noticing the white film that covered one of the woman's eyes as the other seemed to squint to see him. He moved closer, leaning in to her good side. The woman smiled but looked away.

"You've grown up. Look at you, so tall."

"You remember me?"

"Your father spoke highly of you, he was so proud of you."

"Really?

"Yes, really. Come on in here, sit down."

She moved slowly to the house's back door, opening it and holding it as he came inside. It was dark and rather sad inside. Not much light, the windows drawn, and pockets of clutter in the old house dotted each surface.

"Can I get you something to drink?" she asked.

"No ma'am, I'm fine," Tony demurred. "I just came to find out about your work for my father. Uh, Jina was asking about you, so I… wanted to find out."

"Oh, well I been gone a year now," the older woman said. "I only met you and your wife once really, seem like a real nice couple. I was real sad to hear your getting a divorce."

"We're not," Tony corrected her.

"Oh?"

"Yes ma'am, we're not getting a divorce, it was a mistake I made."

The older woman smiled sadly. She sat down in the rocking chair if pondering something complex. "Well now," she said after a time. "I'm glad to hear of some marriages work out. God is still mending hearts. That's real good."

"Ms. Vera, I uh, I came to visit you to find out why you stopped working for my father? Did Sheila fire you?"

"I uh, I retired, that's all," Ms. Vera said abruptly. Agitated, she lifted her watch, bringing her arm close to her face to see the time, before setting her hand back down to grip the arms of the chair.

"You focus on your wife, you build your family," she told him urgently. "Don't go stirring up no trouble."

"What does that mean?" Tony asked, nonplussed. "You can trust me, Ms. Vera. I'm concerned for my father and his health and his uh, business affairs... and what Sheila might do."

"Humph, I see. Well, I ain't got nothing to say. I just, uh, I'm retired," she repeated firmly.

As she stood, the door banged. A young man of about twenty entered, wearing jeans and a t-shirt.

"What the hell are you doing here?"

TONY STOOD UP. The young man was about as tall as he was, but with a clear chip on his shoulder.

"What's he doing here, Ma?"

"He's just visiting. He's Mr. King's son, dear."

"I know who he is."

Tony raised his hands. "Look, I'm sorry, I just came over to, uh, visit your Mom and see how she was doing. Honestly, I was in a car accident a few weeks ago, and I lost some of my memory."

"For real?" The man laughed bitterly. "How convenient, you lost your memory. Your dad's about to die and you can't remember jack. That's a surefire way to get left out of the will, ain't it? Another one bites the dust."

Tony stared. "How did you know that?"

"What you mean how did I know that? It's in the news. Ain't no secret one of the richest Black men this side of the Mississippi about to bite the bullet. People lining up to get a piece of the fortune. You musta lost your memory, and live under a damn rock to boot."

Ms. Vera bristled. "Don't use those words in my house."

"Sorry Ma, but this man is selling some straight bull..."

"I said stop it, Dennis."

The young man kept his gaze fixed on Tony. "Why don't you get out of here? If you ain't bringing the truth of what your daddy gonna give out, then leave, punk." The young man took a threatening stance but Tony didn't flinch. He could feel the anger, he could even identify with it, but it was misdirected. Plus, he knew he could defend himself. He thought it wouldn't come to that with the older woman present, but one never knew. This kid reminded him of himself. Just angry all the time, at everyone and everything: at the very circumstances that kept him in poverty when he had a rich daddy somewhere living the high life. Tony had been mad at life too, then at his father for abandoning him – that is, until he'd met Jina and his life had turned in a completely different direction.

"What is the truth? I may be able to help. I can't make any promises, but I can try to make this right, but I need to know what you know or what you're not willing to share because..."

"All right then, fine," the young man blurted. "Sheila fired Momma because she was gonna tell on her."

"Stop it. That's not true. I told you, I retired." Ms. Vera insisted. Her son nudged her.

"He said he could help, Momma, how bout' we let him try? See what he gone do? What we got to lose, huh?" Dennis looked at Tony with a challenge in his eyes. The head tilted up, fists at his sides itching for a fight, disbelieving anything that came out of Tony's mouth.

Ms. Vera was silent. Defeated, she took a seat, rocking in her chair again, but didn't look at either of them. Her son also took a seat on the edge of the floral sofa. Tony sat finally, ready to listen.

"Yes, please, let me try," he said. "I want to know everything, and I'll do whatever I can to help you, you have my word."

"Yeah right, you make promises just like your old man did - come in here sweet talking my Momma, like she ain't got no sense. She don't need you, or your father's money."

"Isn't he your father, too?"

17

Tony's heart rate increased just thinking about the new revelation as he drove back to the apartment.

Dennis wasn't even thirty years old. God only knew exactly how many other children there were: perhaps his father had been intimate with all his staff, Tony reflected grimly. How many of these offspring even knew King was their father? Of these, how many might now jostle for their rightful inheritance?

Now, the last of the woman his father had seduced, whom one hoped would care for and look after him, had run off all the others simply to ensure no one challenged her authority or knew what she was doing. Sheila King would take the entire fortune if she could. Those seemed to be the facts of the matter. The more Tony had listened, the more his incredulity had grown.

Tony just couldn't bring himself to go to the office at that point. He would eventually, he told himself, but he wanted a quick bite of lunch with Jina and Robby first. Time with them would fortify him to continue working, and he'd like to share with Jina all that he'd learned.

In the meantime, as he drove, he called a number in his

phone. He had been meaning to do so for some time, and now was as good a time as any.

"Tony, good to hear from you," came the voice on the other end. "I've been expecting your call, but I know you've been busy. I thought you might've forgotten that I'm on the payroll. Seriously, you're wise to make use of me. How's everything?"

"I have some questions, Allen. So, you mentioned you're on retainer?"

"Yes, yes of course, whatever you need."

"Have you and my father known each other long?" Tony queried.

"Almost forty years, but - "

"But what?" Tony pressed, almost fearing he shouldn't ask the man too much until he knew more about him.

"Well, it's just that we fell out over that woman," his lawyer responded hesitantly. "The type of woman he tends to align himself with... haven't been the best choices. I can only protect his assets; I can't very well change his relationship picks."

"So you haven't seen him in - how long?"

"It's been a bit," came the reply. "I work mostly with Keith now - and you, of course, up until your accident."

"Do you trust Keith?" Tony wanted to know.

"Well..."

"I'll take that as a no." He knew that lawyer types were rarely at a loss for words.

"All right then." The lawyer chuckled deeply through the phone. "I think you are your father's son: direct, curt. What is it you need?"

"I want my father moved to an undisclosed care facility, top quality, where he can get a second opinion and some testing and treatment for whatever he has. I-I don't have proof," Tony added hurriedly, anticipating the ensuing questions; "but I have cause to believe that she, Sheila, is... harming him."

Tony chose his words carefully. After what he'd learned from Ms. Vera and her son, he now believed Sheila was actively killing his father, deliberately making it a slow death to cover her tracks. At first it had sounded like the craziest thing he'd ever heard, but it was too plausible to be dismissed. With his father dead, she'd inherit a fortune and be free to do whatever she wanted. *Or the two of you could inherit a fortune,* whispered the little voice. *What role do you play?*

He had to be in the vicinity of the truth. If not, how else could Tony explain what he remembered about his father, the urgency his father exhibited when he visited the other day, how easily she drugged him without regard or empathy, how she'd run off the rest of the staff, isolating his father as she did. He hadn't gotten to everything, but it all seemed to make sense. He believed Ms. Vera and her son, who he now knew was in fact his half-brother. As impossible as it was to process that latter part, he would deal with it in time. What cause did they have to lie?

He had to be careful about the multitude of thoughts tumbling through his mind. He might agree if someone called him crazy, because all of this was the most bizarre thing he'd ever been through. He had lots of thoughts, but proof of nothing. As such, he certainly shouldn't be on the phone making such accusations.

"Tony, Tony, are you there? I said, are you being serious?"

"Yes, but no one can know. I-I mean, not Keith, not the media - this can't get out. I need some time. If my Father can get away from her, time will tell if he can improve. It sounds crazy, I know."

"All right, I'll have to get an emergency court order, and you'll have to be his power of attorney," the voice on the other line said slowly. "But we definitely need some proof."

"What if we have a former employee that can attest to

Sheila drugging him? And can you get me a top doctor? I'll get some of the meds, samples, maybe, or pictures of their labels, over to you."

"All right. Now, we really need some kind of urine or blood sample, to see what's in your father's system."

Tony nodded: he had zero idea how that would happen, but he'd try to figure out a way.

"So," Allen continued. "I'll work on this order, Tony. Now, I, ah, didn't want to ask, but what happened with the divorce papers?"

"I'm not divorcing my wife," Tony said sternly - then immediately apologized for his tone. He felt like a broken record, was all. "I'm not getting a divorce under any circumstances," he clarified. "Look, I don't know why I asked you to..."

"You told me that you were only considering it, just as a way to keep from Jina from danger," Allen replied. "You didn't elaborate what danger you meant at the time. Do you think... *this* is what you meant?"

Tony was thoughtful. It did make sense. He was trying to protect Jina and Robby. He'd have a heck of a time getting them back, but he'd rather beg her forgiveness than have something happen.

"I don't know." He really didn't, but hearing it from someone else began to make sense to him now. It made sense when he thought about what Chyna had said at dinner. How Dean had sent Chyna away to Georgia to get her out of harm's way.

It might have worked at least temporarily. Is that what he had thought? Would he really had come up with such a thought on his own?

"Look, how did I ask you to do the divorce papers in the first place?"

"Well, it was quite odd actually: not unheard of, but you asked via text. Granted, something that serious, I should have followed up when you sent it, but I just texted back "okay" and drew them up." Allen sighed. "It's not for me to question my clients, and I'd always thought you hated texting, but I knew you were busy. You don't text me much."

Tony nodded. He did hate texting. At least that hadn't changed.

"I don't think I sent you that, Allen."

"Really? It came from your phone number."

"Yeah, yeah but… I'll get back to you on that. I still have some figuring to do."

"Wow, all that you've said, I really… I hope to God you're wrong about all of this."

"No one wants to be wrong more than I do. Thanks."

Tony pressed the button to end the call, and pulled into a metered parking space outside his building complex. This, he hoped, would force him to keep his visit with Jina brief and get back to work. He needed to have an emergency board meeting and get things in motion regarding his father's estate.

About to enter the Starbucks, he stopped and waved when he saw Jina approaching with Robby, almost a block away. Seeing the two of them after all he'd learned sent a relief like he'd never felt surging through his veins. She spotted him and waved back. He felt like running toward them, but waited impatiently, jostling among quite a few other people on the curb. Jina picked up her pace as she smiled at him, wearing a pair of calf-length purple capris and an oversized shirt tied in a knot at her hip. Her expanding midsection was not yet visible: the baby was, for now, their little secret, although they'd be telling her family soon enough. Sporting plastic shades, Robby was the coolest kid on the block, guzzling the last of the juice from his blue sippy cup without a care in the world. For just a second, Tony closed his eyes to savor the moment of utter contentment.

Suddenly, Jina was pushed down on the ground, and people yelled and ran startled by the commotion.

Tony almost took flight, sprinting toward her. Through the crowd, he could see a man dressed all in black run with the stroller getting farther away before turning abruptly and pushing the stroller hard into an alley. His heart in his throat, Tony turned the corner after him, the man took off, and Tony ran after his son, the stroller moving fast before hitting a trash can with a loud thud. When he got to him, relief surged even as Robby was screaming, not knowing what was happening, jostled by the crash, his tiny sunglasses falling to the ground, but the child was otherwise unharmed.

Quickly, Tony unbuckled him, noticing as he did so a small piece of paper stuck to the child. He pulled it off before grabbing Robby up in his arms and soothing him, whispering to him and rubbing his back. As quickly as he could, he left the alley, surveying everything and searching for the strange man but also for Jina, who thankfully was just turning the corner in search of him. He grabbed her, hugging the two of them close. "He's fine. He is fine," Tony tried to assure her. His arms refused to let them go.

They slowly made their way back to the building where Tony got them situated in the lobby and called the police from his cell phone.

18

When the police arrived, their presence set Jina on edge. She watched them through the silent haze of a burgeoning headache. The questioning officers - two stocky men, one considerably taller than the other - may have thought she wasn't giving as much information as they needed, but the truth was she'd always been wary of them – ever since she'd reported a crime years ago only for nothing to occur and no one to be brought to justice.

The officers asked her about things she hadn't paid attention to; she knew that meant still less chance of any justice. She was almost panic-stricken. She tried to keep Robby on her lap; he kept wiggling away from her, but she kept a death-grip on him. She couldn't let him go and he might have to get used to her clinginess for a bit. She had a mind to lock both of them in their small apartment and never come out again.

"Mrs. King, uh, you've had some kind of assault like this before?" the taller officer queried.

"Almost twenty years ago, yes." She looked over.

"I'm sorry, this must be difficult for you," he replied. "But do you think that someone holding a grudge might have done this? I know you had a pretty high-profile job at the paper."

"I no longer work there." The fact that the past was being brought up at all surprised her. "What on earth would that have to do with this?"

"Nothing, really, ma'am. When we did some research about you, your case and past filings, we thought it worth noting. If your attacker had not been found, they may have struck again – they're likely still out there."

She shrugged. What did she know? She'd had to do a lot of work to move on from that time. She'd survived, and that was all she cared to think about the situation. She couldn't relive her past, and she found it odd for this particular cop to be questioning her about it at all. She remained silent.

"And this note," the officer continued. "Did you receive a note of any sort back then, too?"

"What note?" Jina looked at him blankly.

The officer held out the plastic bag containing the small piece of paper, stark white except for the creepy text: *Get your head out of the clouds and get to work!*

She looked over at Tony, still engrossed in conversation with the other officer. When he glanced at her, he noticed what she had just been shown and she could see the silent apology in his eyes.

"Your husband said this was stuck to Robby's shirt."

She shook her head, "I don't know what it means." She was annoyed that Tony had obviously removed it before she could see it.

The next few minutes were a blur, with the officers finally wrapping up their questions. They mentioned something about gathering security camera footage, then they were gone, with promises to be in touch – only if this were anything like her case long ago, they probably wouldn't. She remembered someone bringing the stroller, but she let Tony take care of it. She held Robby and they were all silent on the way up the elevator and eventually until they were inside the apartment.

She put Robby down for a nap, then rounded on Tony. "Why didn't you tell me about the note?"

"I didn't want to upset you. I was going to tell you, I just didn't want to right then."

"What do you think it's about?"

"I don't know," Tony tried to assure her. "The note looks like it's for me, but how would they know I'd even be there to meet you? Who wants you to return to work, you..."

"I have no idea. What a mess. What did Ms. Vera say?"

"Let's sit first. Do you want some lunch?"

Jina shook her head. She felt too anxious to eat.

"How about some tea?"

She smiled. Despite being a little wary after all that had happened, she knew he was just as concerned as she was.

"Okay, thanks." She took a seat at the kitchen table, watching him make the tea in short order.

"So, first, I think that Sheila is poisoning dad," he began. "That's what Ms. Vera thinks. And she was threatened not to tell by Sheila, so yes, she was fired."

Jina nodded at the news.

"And Dennis, Ms. Vera's son, is my half-brother." Tony casually set the steaming cup in front of her, along with a small wicker tray of lemon wedges, sugar, creamer and a small glass honey pot, before taking a seat across from her.

"You have a brother?" she said incredulously. She held the cup gingerly, letting the warmth into her hands. A part of her was happy that he had extended family, but Tony's pained expression didn't indicate that they'd had an instant bonding experience. It would all take time. In any case, she was in awe of all the information he'd gathered in just a single visit.

"What are you going to do about your father?" she questioned. "He can't stay another minute with her - she might very well kill him."

"I called Allen to see if I can get my father removed from

her care. I am gonna put him in a facility. Have you met Allen?"

Jina shook her head. "I've heard of him. He seems nice enough: no nonsense, serious."

Tony rubbed his brow. "I worry who I can trust, Jina. My father, has all these people after him, his life, his assets, his money..."

"I don't think Vera was," Jina countered. "If they had a child together, then she may truly have cared for him."

"Yes, but apparently she'd be willing to let my Father die and take her thoughts to her grave."

"Maybe Sheila threatened her life," she suggested. "Vera worked for him. She seems a simple woman of meager means, she had no bargaining power except to leave. Maybe he threatened her child?"

"Dennis." Tony looked at her thoughtfully.

"You don't know the agony she might have felt," Jina continued. "She'd do anything to save herself and her son. She threatened Sheila's bottom line, so there's no telling what Sheila could do to her with that money."

Tony pondered. It was hard to understand the motives, but it was true that Vera didn't have much she could use against money and power. Even to tell on Sheila in secret couldn't guarantee Vera complete anonymity. Just one episode of a fictional crime show depicted how easy it was to find out whodunit.

"Maybe Vera came to hate my father," Tony mused. "She seems nice enough, but if my father denied paternity of her child, maybe she grew to hate him too. Maybe she didn't care enough to share information because he didn't show that he cared for her."

Jina was thoughtful. She didn't know the truth or the extent of his father's dealings, but they were complex for sure.

"Maybe your father didn't know," Jina offered. "I can't believe your father is as horrible as he seems."

"I wonder, did I hate him?"

"You didn't," Jina tried to assure him.

"How do you know?" Tony looked at her.

"I believe in you - that you are good. Why take on his affairs?"

"But for a time I was misguided: focused on working for him, forgetting what was important to me."

"Not true."

"Jina, please?"

"No" Jina shook her head. "It isn't true."

"Jina, I want to share an idea with you and then something else. I... I have to tell you something."

Jina was silent. He continued.

"What if I told you I wanted a divorce to keep you and Robby from..."

"From what?

"Out of harm's way."

At first she laughed, but, witnessing the seriousness etched on his face, her own smile faded to doubt and eventually anger. "You would do something so ridiculous?" she exploded. "How could you ever think that us apart is better than us together to fight this thing? I think that would hurt, if that's what you did. The worst kind of hurt you could possibly inflict."

Jina's head was spinning. Risk her feeling like she was losing her mind, all due to some sort of nobility act under the guise of protecting her and Robby? She had set on a course where she gave up her beautiful house, her life, him, her marriage and the safety she'd always felt with him. She'd been willing to exchange it all for complete uncertainty: find a tiny apartment she could afford, move with Robby and pack up everything she loved, all because Tony somehow thought it best for them?

"Why?" He said it as if he couldn't fathom her rage. She was angry at the notion and here she didn't even know if that was what he had done. Right then, it was all a hypothetical he'd just posed, but it made too much sense. Since then, the car accident made him forget his motives, so he'd torn up the divorce papers, moved in and stayed with her. By all appearances, they were a family like before, only under a different, smaller roof.

"I'm trying to protect you and Robby, Jina,"

"You can't - you shouldn't make such a ridiculous decision without even a single piece of input from me! Anything you confront, whatever it may be, you have to believe telling me the truth and putting me in a position to help is better than making up such a horrifying lie. You have to believe that I'm capable of handling the truth."

Tony looked doubtful.

"I'm capable Tony. Trust me, your rejection - your rejection lie, actually, if that's what it was - nearly ended us, and for what? There's still danger and lies and more. Meanwhile, we could've been solid. We wouldn't be wasting time now building us back together if you'd only been truthful!"

Jina didn't realize she was breathing hard until Tony stood and pulled her close. She was taken aback and though she didn't stop him, she felt angry at him at the same time. "I love you."

"I love you and I would do anything, tell you anything, if I thought it meant you and Robby would be protected, from me and from my father's mess. I think I lied to protect you."

"Then, don't you ever do it again," she challenged him. "If you have something you've remembered or found out in the last few days, you tell me. What is it? Trust me enough to tell me, now."

Jina looked him in the eye, searching. Admittedly she was scared about what he would say. She forgave him everything but still the idea that something may be devastatingly irreparable for their marriage and family hung over them like a dark cloud. She wanted to know: not knowing meant they couldn't work on it, whatever it was.

Just as Tony was about to reply, the phone rang. He reached for the phone in his pocket as Jina's phone rang too. She hurried to the stroller, searching for her phone in the diaper bag, and seeing Tish's number, she put it quickly to her ear.

"Jina? Uh, this is Chase, Ms. Alfreah-your Mom, is on her way to the hospital. She's had a heart attack."

19

The last few hours had been a complete blur. Jina packed a few things, barely able to get anything that made sense into her messy duffel bag, and waited in a fog for Dean to come by and take them to the airport. They would be in Macon, Georgia, by later that evening, and at the hospital as fast as their driver could take them. Doctors were removing a blockage, according to Tish. Jina prayed that by the time her mother came out of surgery, she could see her without needing to wait for anything. She prayed that when she arrived, it would be good news.

"Robby is ready, a little sleepy but that might be a good thing. I packed him a couple of snacks and two bottles. You should be good. I checked the website to make sure the ounces limit would make it past security."

Jina nodded mutely: she hadn't even thought about any travel precautions they would have to take. She hadn't been on a plane in some time, and she felt only mildly comforted that Dean and Chyna would travel with her. She put their bags by the door and turned to Tony.

"Your mother is going to be fine. She'll be fine."

Jina nodded, even she buried her face into his chest. Of all the things to throw a monkey wrench into their discussion and plans. Tony was a little relieved that she would be leaving just as things were heating up: as he was just finding out more about his father, as he discovered that Sheila might be able to do his father in with a single lethal dose to the arm, and with Tony powerless to stop her. Regardless, he thought about Jina and all the things she must have been feeling right that minute.

"I'm scared," she murmured. "About my Mom, and about you now that all this is going on. Look, you have to call the police and tell them about Sheila."

Tony nodded against the top of her head. "Please don't worry about this, it will be fine," he told her. "I'm planning to call the authorities, but I can't let her onto what I'm planning until I get my father out of that house. Allen will help me do that."

"What if she... loses it or something?"

"She can if she wants, but it won't change anything."

They both stiffened when the doorbell rang and Tony left her standing in the middle of the kitchen to open the door. He and Dean acknowledged each other curtly, but Jina rushed to hug her brother and they held each other briefly.

"All right, ready?" Dean said matter-of-factly. Tony picked up Robby and handed the child to Dean, who silently grabbed both duffel bags in his other hand and put them on his free shoulder as he moved to the outside of the apartment again, leaving the two of them alone.

"I love you, I will be here when you come back. I'll straighten this out and we can move on."

"Together?"

"Of course, Jina: together." There wasn't any question in his mind despite her look of uncertainty. He meant everything he'd said. "Call me when you get there. I'll be praying for Ms. Alfreah, too."

Jina nodded, holding onto him. He walked them to the

elevator and kissed his wife before kissing Robby goodbye. As the door closed, Tony was surprised at the temporary loss he felt attack his heart. He walked back to the apartment and called the police to see what he could do to speed things up, hoping he could straighten this mess out before Jina returned. That seemed like a tall, even impossible order, but he was going to try his hardest and risk everything to turn things around.

* * *

TONY HAD to do something while he waited to hear from Jina about Ms. Alfreah and their safe arrival in Macon, while also awaiting Allen's call about moving his father, so he got in the car. His mission, he knew, was to find out everything he could about the hours leading up to his accident: something he hadn't thought about for some time.

The drive took him to his Bethesda house, the one he and Jina had purchased a little over a year ago but obviously hadn't actually lived in. Honestly, until he found himself standing before it, he hadn't thought about it at all. Before driving over, he'd scanned pictures of it on the real estate app and read over its numerous amenities, noting the high price tag; but if Jina wasn't there, he saw little need for it at all. It was nice, sort of, despite the overgrowth of the untrimmed yard and cobwebs. He saw past that to the promise it held to reward some TLC.

As he neared the front door, there was a slight stench of something repugnant. Tony couldn't make out what exactly the smell was, but it seemed to hang around the porch in particular. Nonetheless, the porch still looked inviting with wicker furniture that looked new, an outdoor striped area rug and shade from the surrounding trees shielding the porch from the heat of the sun in the warmer months as well as the prying eyes of neighbors across the narrow street.

Looking down at the key chain, Tony searched through the five keys he had on him. He tried two of the newer looking ones, and the door opened on the second he tried. He entered, taking in the vaulted ceilings and lux furnishings: a cobalt blue sofa, loveseat and onyx end tables, with tall tapered candles and matching lamps on each table flanking the sofa and the credenza behind it.

He scoured the place for signs of him and Jina having lived there, but he found none. He didn't feel her presence at all, nor Robby's. They most likely hadn't lived there for even a month before everything fell apart. He suddenly resented the house and all it stood for. There were even parts of it that reminded him of his father's own overgrown fortress. Perhaps he had been trying to emulate his father in some way with a large house, only this house wasn't supposed to be as empty and forlorn as his father's was. It was depressing.

Tony moved quickly to the kitchen and when he opened the fridge it was clear where that foul smell had been coming from: a pack of aging red meat. He immediate got the trashcan, removed the bag and pulled out all the items from the fridge, tossing them and leaving it completely bare. He moved to the kitchen table where there sat a small neat stack of mail. He wondered who would have gotten the mail, unless it was just there from the last time he'd been there.

His eye fell on the folder from a real estate company, with its logo and picture of a new, brightly-lit single family home on the front. Tony opened the folder to find a congratulatory note on their new purchase. "Mr. and Mrs. King... truly spectacular new beginning..." A gift card for a local steakhouse was enclosed, along with more welcome notes, coupons for this and that, and the number for a local maid service. Tony balked. He didn't see anything 'truly spectacular' and certainly nothing to congratulate about his messed up life. He felt sick to his stomach.

Casting the folder aside, he rifled through the mail pile.

One letter was addressed to Jina, only it bore her family home's address. After that, another letter, this one addressed to her apartment where they were together now. He was about to open it but thought better of it. He took the letters, stuffed them into his pocket and took the stairs up to where his office should be. He searched the large space. It had built-in bookshelves, though only a lone shelf held any books. Boxes lined the walls, telling of all that hadn't happened for them: no unpacking, no settling in. An almost-life with his wife that had never manifested itself there. The large desk sat like an island in the middle of the massive room. To his surprise, the computer woke when he touched the mouse. For some reason, he checked the trash folder and clicked the 'put back' link on the file, restoring a letter he must've written titled 'RandJ'.

Tony opened it and read it three times. Finally, he had everything he needed to know. Everything his memory was missing was right there for him, in black and white. His eyes clouded with tears as he read but he managed to blink them away. He had all the answers. He hadn't asked her for a divorce and his entire life made more sense. The situation was still unfathomable, but reading his own words told him what he needed to know. He wiped his face, feeling a sigh of relief. The car accident wasn't an accident. He could have very well died that night if God hadn't meant for him to live: meant for him to have this second chance and cheat the death that others intended for him.

When Tony's phone rang, he took a deep breath and saw Jina's name in the identification text. He swiped right and breathed a sigh of relief to hear her voice.

"She's gonna be okay."

Tony breathed a second hard whoosh of pent up relief and smiled into the phone. "Baby, great, that's so great."

"Come what, come home?" Tony questioned not hearing her next statement, still soaking in the relief that Ms. Alfreah's prognosis was good before he heard that Jina was insisting she and Robby return home, immediately.

"Come home. No, no." Tony stood up alarmed. "Not yet." He couldn't have her home, not yet. "Just stay, just a few days, help Tish get everyone settled, start your Mother's rehabilitation if she needs that. I am fine," he assured her.

"I – I remember some things. I can't wait to see you baby, but please, J. Give me a few days."

He tried to assure her that everything was okay, but considering all that he told her right before they'd got the call about Ms. Alfreah, he didn't want to add more stress. He still needed more time to get things straightened out. He had the truth this time, not just some silly uncertainties. This time he knew what he was up against. To his relief, what Jina thought about him was the truth.

As they spoke, her need to get home to him seemed to lessen as he continued to assuage her fears. He told her again and again how much he loved her, even as he rushed her off the phone. He hurriedly made copies of the items on his computer and opened a separate cloud account to store a few more documents there: password protected, of course. Though he hesitated, he gave himself just a day, and scheduled an email to post sometime within the next forty-eight hours. He hated to give it to her unawares, without him present while she read it, but considering the fallout and the mess right then, he wouldn't waste any more time getting it to the person he'd originally intended before everything went south. Ultimately, Jina was the one person who needed to read it most.

Tony was just taking another look around the house when the phone rang again. He answered immediately when he saw Allen's name. He rushed down the steps as he listened, ready to be done with that house and the entire scene.

"Your father is going to be moved tonight," came Allen's

voice. "We have a court order and there will be police protection. You might want to be there, too."

"I'll be there - thanks Allen, thank you." Tony hung up the phone. He had to go to the authorities with what he knew straight away, to bring the woman who was out to kill his father - and him, he now knew - to justice.

20

It was late when Jina and Chyna returned to the Alton home. A spread of pastries, fruit and mini sandwiches was laid out, and lots of coffee and tea seemed to flow constantly. Despite being a tad hungry, Jina headed upstairs first to look in on Robby: sound asleep in a place that had become familiar to him. She didn't disturb him. He'd had enough excitement, from rushing out of Virginia amidst the incident that had scared her to death, to plane-hopping back to Macon where he could be with his cousins once again. He was surely feeling the stress through her, too, as she worried incessantly about everything from her mother's health to someone taking Robby away from her, as well as the safety of the husband she'd left alone. She wanted to hold Robby, and she wished for Tony's strong arms to hold her; but she didn't have Tony, and she wouldn't bother Robby out of her own need. She wanted to go home soon, and he should rest up for the trip back.

She left the room quietly, leaving the door slightly ajar as she moved back downstairs. Everything was eerily quiet. Earlier they'd all been so nervous about Ms. Alfreah's condition, but now her mother was talking, even up walking around her hospital bed. Seeing her with her own eyes was tremendously comforting to Jina, even watching her doing the most mundane things she would usually take for granted. The way Tish had described her mother had initially panicked Jina, but those first few hours were critical, according to her cardiologist, and had made the difference in her mother's recovery, along with the surgery that removed the blockage.

Doctors thought she looked great, considering the ordeal, and Jina managed to pull herself together. Truth be told, her mother seemed upbeat, amazingly lucid and even a bit more energetic since she'd had her surgery than when she'd last seen her mother just weeks ago. Either the surgery had done miracles for her energy levels or the drugs were giving her an added dose of energetic display. Dean and Tish stayed at the hospital a little longer, while Jina had driven herself and Chyna back to the Alton home.

When she turned around with her cup of tea, Chyna was there, handing her a plate.

"Do you want this warmed?" Chyna asked her after she finished adding ingredients to her tea.

Jina shook her head, taking the plate. "No, no, should be fine, Chyna. Now, stop waiting on us. You don't work here. Thanks," she added belatedly. She popped a mini blueberry muffin into her mouth before they left the kitchen to sit in the den.

The television played quietly in the background. It had become something to stare at, helping to keep eyes occupied and minds a bit numb as everyone filed in and out over the last two days, taking their turn at the hospital keeping watch over Ms. Alfreah.

"Your Mom looks really good, J," remarked Chyna. "She's gonna be fine. She'll have to change her diet some, maybe do a little more exercise, but she looked so good."

"Thank you." Jina smiled sadly. "Thanks so much for being here. Having you around to translate the doctor's overly complex spiel these last few days has really made a huge difference."

"I'm so glad I could be here. You know I love you guys."

Jina sipped more of her tea and smiled behind her mug. "Dean was so worried. I'm glad he calmed down a little. His anxiety just amplified my own."

"Hmm, probably because you two are so much alike."

"What?" Jina shot back. "Uh no, he's way worse."

Chyna laughed. "I don't think so. You're almost identical."

"How so?" Jina was curious. She knew her and Dean were the most similar, but truth was they all acted alike depending on the circumstance.

"Well like now. You're clearly going through something, but you're trying to act all cool. Do you want to talk about it? Before you try to deny it, I can see it's more than just your mother's recent illness. Are you and Tony gonna be okay? The news coverage over his father seems to be growing. How is he?"

Jina chewed another pastry, setting her plate on the coffee table in front of her. She shrugged. She didn't want to talk about Tony even though she could hardly keep her mind and thoughts off of him and what issues he currently was confronting at any given moment, back in Virginia without her. What did he find out about his father? Did he uncover any more siblings? Was he able to get his father away from Sheila? Would she do something to harm him in the process? Would the police accompany Tony and help if Sheila pulled some stunt? All manner of questions ran through her mind, and new questions seemed to form hourly.

"So, Tony believes that his evil stepmother may be slowly killing his father," she admitted.

"What, what? Jina that is absolutely crazy. How, why?"

"To get her money faster?" Jina hedged. Was there really a good explanation beyond the large payout that Jina could think of? She really didn't know why, only that it was the craziest thing she'd ever heard of, not to mention the scarier thought of what Sheila might do if she discovered she'd been found out and that her little plan was about to be interrupted.

"Oh my God, you must be so worried about Tony - and his father, for that matter?"

"I am. I may leave tomorrow, but he's urged me to let this stuff die down a bit first. It's just that I want to be with him when he finds out the extent of the damage she may have done to his father's health. What if she accelerated his illness beyond any rescue? Even though Tony's known she might be doing this for a few days now, he's had to wait almost this entire week for a court order and a judge to rule to get his father out of there. Can you imagine?"

Telling someone else the story was a relief, unburdening her of the magnitude of the secret, but it also crystallized the urgency of the matter.

"Do you think it's true about King's, uh, children?" Chyna questioned.

It was the million-dollar question. "Unfortunately I do: Tony has already encountered one," she confided. "His name is Dennis and he lives right in Alexandria with his mother. He's all of about twenty-five. His mother worked for Mr. King for several years."

Chyna raised her eyebrows. "Wow. And what if there are more?"

"There likely are," Jina acknowledged. She sipped her tea, the silence between them stretching on as they both focused on the news of the day. When a story came on talking about the very man they'd just been discussing, Jina sat frozen to the spot, unable to tear her eyes away from the anchorwoman's face.

Out of the corner of her eye, she saw Chyna scramble for the remote on the coffee table, pointing it at the large television to turn it up.

Today, a northern Virginia court ordered that millionaire

real estate guru Alex King, who hasn't been seen in public for over a year, be removed from his wife's care to an undisclosed location. He is believed to be at an area Immediate Care Facility for medical attention and evaluation. The court ruled in his eldest son's favor that Anthony King will become his temporary guardian while an investigation gets underway.

The elder King's wife, socialite and former nurse Sheila King, is believed to be pregnant with King's son, but rumors continue to circulate that the child is that of an employee at the firm and not King's own child, which would be one of many apparent heirs to the King fortune.

An Alexandria judge will later rule on who will execute the conservatorship of the elder King, which will include direction of his estimated one billion dollars in real estate properties, part ownership of the Washington Rebels Football Team, and other assets. The judge is expected to rule by the end of next week. In other news...

JINA LOOKED AWAY from the television. As the louder commercials began, Chyna thoughtfully turned the volume back down to a tolerable level.

"I had no idea she was a nurse," Chyna said at last.

Jina shrugged her shoulders: "It's news to me, too."

"You know, this is like one of those horrible nursing stories I heard about in my schooling. The elder abuse that goes on by these private duty nurses is horrifying, Jina. I - I can't even bear to think about it."

Jina nodded. "It must be hard. Don't even think about her, though. You're one of the good nurses. Just, just put it out of your mind."

"But, listen, as a nurse, she would know exactly how much of a dosage to give Tony's father," Chyna pointed out. "His health would deteriorate, yes, but unless extensive tests are run, no one would be any the wiser that she'd inflicted that pain. It's going to be so hard to prove that she intentionally did something so horrifying to him, if she's giving only trace amounts at a time."

The pain in Chyna's voice wasn't helping Jina's nerves. All that she said was true, but as someone with no medical experience Jina hadn't thought about it. Being a nurse - former or current, whatever Sheila's claim - gave everything a whole different meaning and a new sense of urgency. Jina stood and searched for her phone, wondering if Tony had called her, but when she finally located it there were zero messages. She sat back down, feeling defeated.

"And she's pregnant, Jina?"

"Okay, okay!" Jina almost yelled, her tone of voice startling Chyna. "I'm sorry, just uh… can you find some HGTV or something? I'll watch a chess match at this point - just please turn the channel."

The worry was getting to her and a thought that she had previously entertained now returned full throttle. "Listen Chyna, I have a favor to ask you."

"Of course - anything."

"Will you bring Robby home when you guys come? I'm gonna… I'm gonna go home."

Jina stood to pace. While she was nervous, she had to get to her husband, despite his insistence that she stay away for a few more days. Time was up. The news hadn't helped her nerves, but with her Mother stable, she now felt okay leaving. She had to see Tony with her own eyes. She had to make sure he knew he could count on her and that she was a full fifty percent of the team they made. Their last conversation had demonstrated what lengths he would go to to protect her.

"Yes, of course, but Jina, what will I tell Dean and Tish? They'll kill me for letting you go by yourself."

"I, I have to. I just… I'll be fine. I'll call as soon as I touch down."

Jina had made up her mind. Getting out of the house was

the only thing she had to do; she'd figure the rest out when she got the airport. She searched her phone for a ride share, then for a flight to DC, before repacking her bag.

Though she was kind of leaving Chyna in the lurch, she knew she'd either call Dean and Tish as soon as Jina was out the door or call Tony, so he could be on the lookout for her. Either way, Jina only had so much time to make it all happen. Ready to go, in record time for once, she hugged her best friend, now sister-in-law, and hopped into the car that pulled up to the house. She waved goodbye, assuring Chyna one last time that she would be fine. She would be, she told herself, as soon as she was able to lay her eyes on Tony.

21

Remembering the faces of the doctors glancing from his father back to him, Tony felt browbeaten. Their expressions had been disbelieving, skeptical even. Though he'd been assured that he couldn't possibly have known, he still felt some accusation in their eyes. His father's current critical condition was not only preventable, their glances said, but it was somehow also his fault. "That's not what they said." Allen had told him again and again.

The group of doctors included some of the top minds in the country. There was a specialist for human brain functioning; a Parkinson's specialist, which his father was believed to have; and an elder abuse attorney, one of only a hundred in the United States who was also a practicing physician. Tony couldn't believe the quality and depth of knowledge within the room that Allen had pulled together. An independent ICU nurse had also been contracted for the next few days: as long as his father needed.

Tony considered the whole experience as he drove robotically back to the apartment for the night. He felt both hope and fear from their findings. Their grim faces didn't help, but at least his father's wife couldn't inflict any more pain. Hopefully his father wouldn't have to return to her care, ever. Tony planned to make sure of that, and had consulted Allen about how on earth they could ensure it. The evidence had to be stacked against her.

"I have to get this extended," Tony recalled telling Allen, whom it turned out he did recognize in person despite not having known him from his voice.

"You will," Allen had assured him. "The doctor's reports can be submitted in evidence. Neglect, over-medication, falsifying reporting to the main care attendants and even your father's other doctor could all be found duplicitous. There are bruises on his arms, and an unattended pressure sore that might be infected. All told, this could send her to jail for life. We will push for the harshest penalties possible. We just have to wait a few days to see if this medication wears off and measure your father's cognitive function, but the brain wave testing looks really good."

"How can I get her to take a paternity test?" Tony hadn't wanted to ask that question, but the thought of it never left him.

Allen looked as if he'd seen a ghost.

"So the employee, at the firm is... *you?*"

"No, it's not me," Tony said, confused. "It's not – I mean, I don't..."

"You don't remember?"

"It's not me!" Tony had insisted, but his declarations didn't hold water without concrete evidence. Tony thought about all of this as he drove home. He was mentally and physically exhausted.

When he arrived home and walked in the door, he felt like he was seeing things. Maybe he'd had another accident, died and was currently in heaven, for all he knew. Candles illuminated the table. Next to the stove, Jina, decked out in a skimpy Kimono-style silk robe and barefoot, was stirring something that smelled heavily. Tony gave himself a shake. He knew that couldn't possibly be, as there was no way Jina would leave her ailing mother to come home - and if she did, she certainly wouldn't be feeling domestic, or romantic for that matter, considering the last few days.

Still, the image wouldn't leave, and the smell was so real, it made his mouth salivate; but he wasn't really hungry for food at all. Seeing her looking so beautiful brought about a different kind of hunger.

"I'm going crazy, I'm hallucinating, is this a dream?"

He turned to set down the papers and folders he carried and shut the door. When arms came around his waist, his heart beat faster and he just stood there, rooted to the spot.

"Jina, baby, what are you doing here? I thought - I thought I was freaking losing it."

"You're not crazy. I'm right here," she whispered. She dabbed a tissue to her nose, sniffling. Even though the kitchen was mostly dark except for the ambient lighting, there was enough light for him to see her eyes, glassy with tears. He kissed her tears away.

"I'm still so annoyed with you," she gasped. "I got the letters, the ones you sent via email and these" - she gestured to the top of the microwave – "and as annoyed as I am about your stupid little plan to protect me, I can't be, not right now. Maybe never again. I made the decision to come home before I got the letters, but I read them on the plane. I was crying so hard that a member of the cabin crew came over several times to make sure I was all right. A child in the seat in front offered me her teddy bear." She laughed and cried at the same time.

Tony listened intently, wanting to laugh too, but he didn't. The seriousness of the situation trumped her silly story. He took a deep breath, putting his forehead against hers. All at once, he picked her up, her legs around him and just held her, staring into her eyes.

"Stop - put me down!" she exclaimed. "You should not be picking me up - what about your back?"

"I'm fine."

At the very last minute, in their perfect house that was now a shell of nothingness - an empty vessel of nice things but no love - he had decided to send the letters to her. He could not describe the relief now that he knew the truth and that everything was finally out in the open.

"You didn't trust me, Tony."

His head shot up. "I didn't trust myself," he said seriously. "I trusted you to wait until I figured out what on earth I was doing. To fix it, without dragging you through it right on the heels of your father's death, then Dean's issues with the Hardigs', nearly getting killed. The fact that this letter even exists is a testament to your influence."

Tony rubbed the frown lines from her forehead before continuing. "Your father's illness and eventual death scared you into documenting all the awesome milestones of your life, from Robby's walking to his first words, and your pregnancies, through your blog, through all of those years at the paper. You were always journaling, always writing big stuff, little stuff, even just general observations. With all that was going on with both of us, all that I had to keep track of, my father's mess made me crazy - so I started to document that stuff too. I can tell you it wasn't nearly as detailed and some of what you would write. It often felt like gibberish and nondescript junk, to be honest; but at least I wrote something down. I had to have you in mind through it all, influencing me."

Tony breathed hard. He released the revelations that came to him in the days since they'd been together. Considering he hadn't known whom to trust, he resolved then and there that he should first start trusting his wife with everything: with his scheme, with the truth. He'd wanted to wait to give her context with the letter, but considering the scare before she'd left, he just didn't want to take that chance. He set her down on the counter and gently removed the letters from her hand, setting them aside. He continued to stare at her, even as her lips beckoned his. He stole a kiss.

"I don't want to belabor this, but there is one thing I need you to hear."

"What?" he said.

"Don't ever do that to Robby and I again. Now, tell me about your father, how is he doing?"

"Humph," he smirked, shaking his head. He tried to dismiss the thoughts of everything: to let his mind go blank as he relished a closeness with her that he hadn't felt in what seemed like an eternity. He shook his head and blew out a breath. "Well, I could have alienated everyone, just like him. I could have been just one more life-sucking leech on a long list of crazy, no good, heartless people who intended to do my father in," he went on. "He's sick - they won't know exactly how much damage she's done in the last year, with everyone unawares. I could have turned out like him."

"And you didn't," she said quickly.

"I could've been," he said again.

"And you are not. Period," Jina repeated firmly.

Tony smiled. "You've only been gone a few days and it felt like an eternity. Is Robby sleeping?"

Jina shook her head. "When Dean and Chyna return, they will bring him. They should be coming tomorrow, I hope."

"Of course, of course." He lifted her chin, refocusing his attention on the delicate lace of her robe. "So, in this little romantic set up, did you actually intend to start something? Because that's what it looks like."

Jina smiled. "Well, it wasn't my original game plan, but reading the letter on the way over, seeing you, and remembering how much I love you... well, sometimes plans change. Add by the way, having you beside me every single night is like buying a cupcake just to look at. Why on earth have it if you're not going to eat it?"

"I'm a cupcake now?" Tony's eyes changed when she

scooted to the edge of the counter, wrapping her arms around his neck. For her to initiate things encouraged him where it didn't take much at all. He'd been waiting for this moment for what seemed like an eternity.

"I've been waiting, Jina. I've been trying to give you space, to stay away, but I want and need you. I always have, and I always will."

"You have," she replied. "You've been so patient and I appreciate it so much, I appreciate your telling me everything and giving me the time and space to process all that has happened, and..."

"And you deserve someone better than..."

"Shut your mouth and give me a kiss," Jina admonished.

He laughed but quickly obliged, kissing her the longest he could remember since his accident and relishing every second. She leaned forward as he pulled back, slowly. He picked her up again, and as he turned, he remembered to turn off the burner that simmered under something she'd made. He managed to hold her with one hand as he lifted the lid to the pot, smiling at the deep brick red color of the sauce.

"My favorite."

She nodded. "You remember?"

"A few things I haven't lost: my ability to cook, my love for food and my deep desire for you, my wife."

"Well I also would not want to burn up all my efforts on the spaghetti – it's about the only thing I know how to make at all, so it definitely shouldn't go to waste while we're, uh, busy?" She buried her face in the crook of his neck, laughing.

"If something is gonna burn, I'd prefer it to be the bed sheets."

"Let's go then," Jina said, her warm hands caressed his bald head and placed kisses on the side of his face.

Tony closed his eyes momentarily, reveling in the feel of her touch, her breath. For a time, he'd thought he would never experience anything like this again, and now there he was with a second chance. If only his father could be so lucky: recover, perhaps even have the opportunity to meet his grandson, then hang on long enough to meet his other grandchild in the coming months. Would that be too much to ask of God?

Dismissing the current woes that tried to dog him, Tony focused on the good: a beautiful and sexy wife, his only wife, his only baby mama - thank God - and his forever life-partner. As they undressed one another, he never took his eyes off Jina, even as they laughed, talked and shared intimacy. For the rest of the night they recommitted to their marriage, love and their intent to move forward, together.

22

For the umpteenth time that afternoon, Sheila shooed away the man nibbling her ear in a very poor attempt at being romantic. Her plans were crashing around her and the man before her wanted to get it on, as they'd done a hundred other times before. She wasn't feeling it, not right then – heck, maybe not ever again, not when she was on the verge of losing everything. She'd worked so hard, and now it was collapsing around her. She scrolled through several emails, looking for past communication from a specific reporter that would help her before the media could paint her into something she couldn't evade indefinitely.

Feeling the man's hot breath once more, she pushed him away for what she hoped was the last time. "Could you please just stop? Damn, I need air to think and a little space." She put up a hand to stop him, as he had that weird look in his eye: that murderous gleam. She didn't know if she could put it past him, but she didn't have time for that right now. "Look," she kissed him on the lips for good measure, hoping to reset him as usual - "have you, uh, seen the news yet?"

The man shook his head. "I think better after we, uh, you know… so now you're playing hard to get, huh? The other night and all the times before, you seemed much more, how should I say... agreeable?"

"Well, in case you haven't noticed, the one person in charge of everything we need to make this thing go is no longer here," she snapped.

"THEN ABORT THE MISSION, or that part of it. Surely you gave him enough that he can't possibly start babbling anything other than nonsense?"

"Are you kidding? We are not just gonna give up. Now, instead of mauling me, think – think! We need a new plan already. You do not get to abort the mission. Do you hear me? You do not get to just forget about everything."

"What are you talking about?" The man stood up, away from her. "This train is off the rails, Sheila. The best way to fix this is to let it go."

"Let it go?" Sheila stuttered.

"Yes."

"The hell are you talking about? I worked too hard!"

"You had help! You act like you did everything by yourself. And what did you do, exactly? Slip the old man some drugs, and spread lies. Hey, I'm the one down there working everything and figuring out the accounting system, siphoning funds gradually for the last year. You know your problem, Sheila, is that you're stupid. You forget I helped you. It's not my fault you tried to kill the old man and then it backfired on you. Now what? What's the plan? You could have moved money a little at a time, like I told you, like I was doing..."

"You talk about me being slow," she hissed back. "You're the one who's slow! I don't have the time to wait for your stupid methods. How long have you even been there? You got Tony to hire you, then what? You've done nothing."

"No, but your greed is the reason it's not working for you. Your fault." The man fixed his suit.

"Isn't it funny how I'm the only one facing jail time right now? That is, if they find me, of course. I've disappeared once, I can disappear again." Sheila pushed the laptop away in disgust.

"I could face jail time too, you know," he countered. "There may be evidence out there, implicating me."

"Like what?"

"I don't know. I tried to cover my tracks - and you still haven't answered me about the paternity, by the way. I want to know, now. Did you even do the test? Tell me."

"Really, now? Well, maybe yes, maybe no," She laughed and then looked him up and down before sucking her teeth. "My scheme is so good, I got everyone believing whatever the heck I want them to." She laughed menacingly.

The man's face changed. "I thought we were just - just fooling around, Sheila. You told me you were on birth control."

She shrugged and he didn't like it. She knew how much he hated her demeaning nature.

"Stop jerking me around, you bitch."

Sheila scooted out of the way when he lunged for her. She whirled around to escape him again, but instead of lunging for her a third time, he pushed her. Her head hit the end of the door, and the impact sobered her immediately. Before she could retaliate, he'd rushed at her, his hands clawing at her clothes, grabbing handfuls of her blouse: the lapels, then the long pieces that hung in a bow. In a moment they were undone and he wrapped them around her throat, pulling before she could understand that he meant to hurt her for real this time. She struggled against him, but the fabric only grew tighter.

"Stop it - " His eyes changed. She couldn't breathe. She clawed at him and he dragged her, shaking her. A gasp whooshed out of her lungs, but she couldn't get more air in, "Did you sleep with him, did you?" he snarled. "Is the child really Tony's?"

"I can't - " Sheila begged, her voice barely a whisper as she struggled.

"Tell me the truth," he sneered.

"I can't. Please."

"This is what you get. You should not have lied, Sheila. We could have had it all. I don't want no baby, but if it's his, I'll be damned if he'll raise it. He can't have everything, he can't... the bastard gave him everything, left him everything, more than me, we're equals." A tear snaked down the man's cheek as he wheezed with rage. His hands contracted and he looked at them, seeming almost surprised at what he was doing. Still he felt nothing.

Sheila struggled against him, her hands scratching his wrists, before they fell away as she went limp. The man held her as the lead weight of her body forced him down with her, both of them sliding to the floor.

When he stood, he backed away. Sheila's eyes rolled to his but she didn't say anything, and the man above her just stared back at her, unmoving.

As if coming back to himself, he adjusted his clothes and brushed off his knees. He fixed his suit as if he'd just gotten dressed, checking his appearance.

"Keith" she said one last time, before the door closed.

23

After what could only be described as an extraordinary night, Tony drifted in the afterglow: conscious, but not fully awake, not yet. Thoughts of Jina's warm, welcoming body cloaked him like a soft blanket. Throughout the night he'd marveled at how her body had changed, how beautiful she was with his child. Now, he was content to remain still, in bed, unbothered by everything. There was so much to confront, yes; but that always brought panic and thoughts of darkness - so much so that in between wanting to get up and make Jina breakfast, his heart started to race, as he sank back into what at first seemed like sleep, only without rest.

Behind his closed lids, a smoky haze infiltrated the scene unfolding behind his eyes. Pungent and acrid, it choked him, and he was pushed from behind into still deeper darkness. At first he began to toss and turn; his arms felt pulled in either direction, stretched beyond human capability like rubber bands, until something snapped. His back hurt, he felt weighted down and he thrashed, trying to get free. Rolling in the sheets, he was near drowning. He took a deep breath, only it wasn't deep enough. Jina's smiling face appeared before him, only she was being pulled away from him, her face now turning from calm and serene to consternation mirroring his own. She was being pulled by someone, taking her... Her hands reached for his and he reached forward desperately to grasp her but could never make contact. The more he stretched to get to her, the further away she moved from him. And then she was gone.

Tony managed a small deep throated cry aloud, wrenching himself awake. He sat up, breathing hard, and looked over at the small mound of covers beside him – but when he pulled them back, it was empty. Jina really was gone.

Fully awake in an instant, he detangled himself from the covers, tripping as one wrapped itself around his ankle. He hopped free, out of the bedroom door, racing toward the front door of the apartment.

Suddenly he heard the keys jangle and the door opened to reveal Jina, holding a small brown paper bag and a tray with two tall white cups.

He rushed to her, took the bag and the coffee from her fingers gently and placed them on the table before pulling her close. "You scared me half to death. Why didn't you tell me where you were going?"

"I just went downstairs to the building's Starbucks," she answered, laughing. "I didn't even leave the building. There were all kind of people milling about. I thought I'd be OK."

"Jina, do you recall what happened before you went to your mother's?" Tony asked with some irritation. "There were people milling about on the street in broad daylight then, too. We have to do things a little differently now, J. *Please.*"

"Okay, okay, I'm sorry." She rested her head against his chest and he pulled her tighter, praying for their nightmare to end soon.

They went about the rest of their morning at home: cleaning up a bit, drinking their coffee and eating the croissants she'd brought. Tony checked the news feed and a number of messages. He needed to call an emergency board meeting, so he set that in motion by emailing his father's secretary. Only an hour had passed before Tony's phone rang.

"Your father is asking for you. Come."

The words propelled Tony with a new wave of urgency. He uttered something like *Okay* or *I'll be there* - he really didn't remember - as Jina watched his every move expectantly. He still gripped the phone as Jina moved closer to him and touched his arm, her eyes expectant.

"Your father?"

"He's asking for me, Allen said." Tony's eyebrows rose as he set the phone aside.

She nodded. "I'm going, too," she uttered.

"Jina -" he warned, trying to sound stern, but knowing it was futile.

"Tony?" she replied, also in warning.

The two of them had a short staring contest but when she put her hands on her hips, he put his hands up immediately in surrender. He couldn't argue, anyway: he desperately wanted her with him, despite his initial concerns. If there was any way to ensure her safety then it was to keep her as close to him as possible. He reflected that if Jina's dream back at her sister's house had been anything like his own dream earlier that morning, he felt more empathetic with her fears. He didn't ever want to experience the nightmare of her somehow being drawn away from him again. He would also welcome her moral support, and the calm she brought him.

With that decided, Tony's mind quickly returned to considering what he might encounter when he visited a talking, less under-the-influence version of his father. Who knows what the man had to say, after all this time? A thousand pressing questions would have to wait. Was his father even lucid? How much time did he have left? What kind of quality of life would he have after all of this? Could the doctors even tell about the longer-term outlook? How much damage had

Sheila done to him? Could he even help them, him, Allen, and the authorities understand how Sheila had done what she did? Did his father even know why? How could they prove she did something?

Did his father know about the results of his own infidelities: about how many children lay in the wake of his constant affairs? That was the question of all questions. Had he grown to care more about the later children, or would they too grow up without a father, much the same way Tony himself had? Did they even know their father was a millionaire, with the means to care for them but no desire to do so? Wasn't that really the one thing that bothered him the most out of everything?

"I'm done in the shower - come on, get ready," Jina prodded him. Tony looked down at her, dazed. He hadn't moved from the spot: he hadn't heard her leave, nor heard the shower running. Absently, he moved to the bathroom as his thoughts continued to consume his mind. They got ready silently. Tony was hesitant at first. He had more clothes in the closet now that he'd been there and been to work several times. His first day seemed to come back to him: while he'd wanted to impress his father and the business people he would encounter, he resisted the urge to dress up. He was done playing that role. It cost too much to play those games, and he didn't feel any of it: no more mindless loyalty to a man that claimed to be a father but had put zero time into the act of becoming one. Money be damned. Making a decision to go with something more comfortable, Tony opted for a clean, crisp long-sleeved dress shirt, a pair of nice slacks and some leather loafers.

Though he was still thinking about everything, he gripped Jina's hand. Her patient presence helped him remain calm even as he got the car, drove to the private immediate care facility and took the elevator to the top floor of the otherwise nondescript building blending in with so many other

Arlington high-rise offices and condominiums. No-one would be the wiser that his father or any other rich, ailing business mogul was housed there. It didn't even have a marquee featuring its name. Unidentifiable.

Feeling like he was teleporting himself down the hall, Tony walked to see the man who'd nearly been killed at the hands of his own too-young, propelled by greed wife, and abandoned by his employees and other so-called comrades. Nobody had cared, then or now, and that made Tony resentful. For some reason, he was the only one there now, left trying to pick up the pieces.

What on earth would Alex King have to say, Tony wondered, about the missing months of his life? How to fix everything that from Tony's perspective seemed completely irreparable, not to mention way too little, way too late?

24

"Son?"

The voice sounded small, distant, as if coming from somewhere far away, not from the bed marooned in the center of the mostly bare space where Alex King lay.

As curious as Tony was, he was also unsure about what his father would dare ask him to do. How could he ever clean up the mess he'd made of everyone's lives, including children who might never even know him at all?

Hearing the raspy whisper of the man on the bed, Tony felt a pull at first, and moved forward quickly.

"His left arm is a paralyzed," the nurse said quietly. "There may be some involuntary spasm, but due to the neuropathy and overmedication, he's not able to lift it." She adjusted the pillow. For someone that had just meant his father days ago, the nurse exhibited a surprising level of care. Tony found this so strange to see, but only because it was his father. Nurses, did the same for everyone, complete strangers, every single day. But his resentment clouded his ability to see his father as a human first: he had to keep reminding himself of that fact.

The nurse quickly finished her ministrations before smiling and nodding at Tony and Jina as she left.

Tony rushed forward, taking the side with the still functional arm that reached toward him. He perched on the edge of the bed and grabbed it, cradled it, resting it on his knee. At first it felt odd. It seemed almost intimate, and up until then he couldn't remember any act of affection from his father, not even a hug. Granted, Tony didn't recall almost twelve months of his life, most of which was only filled in by the writings he'd left. To remember their lack of more personal contact felt painful.

His father's grip on Tony's hand wasn't strong, and the effort of holding it seemed to wind him: the hand went limp in Tony's own. He gently set it between them. He continued holding his father's hand as tears clouded his eyes.

"It's okay, it's okay,"

"Lemme speak," came the faint voice.

Tony nodded.

"It's been a while since I said anything so I got a lot to get out before, before..." Alex looked over at the doctor who stood on the other side of the bed. The doctor shrugged, and Alex returned his eyes to Tony.

"I loved your Mother, of all the women, I loved her," he continued. That's why I chose you, asked you to help me. I had no idea I'd embroil you in a mess."

His father drew a breath. "Here is what I want you to do. Allen will help you. Get these papers signed before I, I may be declared incompetent."

"But you're not -" Tony began.

"It won't stop them from trying to paint such a picture," Allen chimed in grimly.

"So after you are in charge, you will liquidate my assets, sell off the properties and if you still have any left, gift them to the original owners," his father went on. "Whatever children have my DNA then, at least one million dollars each, and the rest into an endowment fund for their children and their children's children - or divide it up between them equally. I want you to give ten million to your mother's alma mater, Howard University."

Listening to his instructions, Tony was surprised by his generosity - but it hurt too. His mother had barely finished at Howard, with a child on her hip and no real money to do anything. He swallowed several times. Jina squeezed his shoulder. She felt solid and capable against him and he was able to sit just a tad taller. He couldn't believe this man's seemingly cold heart would consider his mother at all. He struggled with trying to reconcile all that had happened, all that his father was asking him to do, and all that his father had done to bring about the current situation in the first place. He wanted to do the right thing. At least he had some help in Allen, in the doctors and most importantly, now that the truth of everything was open between them, in Jina.

"The rest of the money for you and your family," his father concluded.

"I don't want it."

Tony couldn't believe the words that came out of his mouth, but the truth was that this whole time he'd wanted to say something so full of rejection. He didn't feel it as strongly as he said it, but now he knew that he might have even practiced it for such a moment. The thing was, he'd always imagined his father upright when he said the words, that they'd be eye-to-eye and sparring in some heated argument. This wasn't that fight, however. The man before him was fighting to live, and Tony just was warring with himself: battling his unwillingness to forgive the man and the situation before him. He needed to let it go.

"Son, please?" his father said, a touch of pleading in his voice.

"Are your businesses even legitimate?" Tony asked coldly.

"I said I don't want it. I... can't." He wanted no part of his father. Not anymore.

"What is - what is he asking?" Jina asked.

"Nothing, nothing. Can we just have a minute?"

"Yes, of course." Jina hesitated a moment, but left them alone in the room. Tony looked back at his father.

"Your wife is so beautiful," Alex remarked.

Tony wasn't even sure why the comment rubbed him the wrong way, but his jaw twitched in annoyance.

"Listen to me, do you know that your so-called wife tried to pawn *your* child off on *me*?" he exploded. "I almost gave up everything trying to fix your mess, a mess I have nothing to do with, other than to be the only one concerned with your pathetic life and trying to honor your dying wishes. I was in a car accident - I nearly died. Do you understand me?"

Even as he told his father everything, a rapid fire spewing of events over the last two months, a part of him knew how little it mattered. What was his father going to say or do after the fact? Tony realized he may be telling him to see if the old man ultimately cared about him. He was still vying for some sort of sympathy, an ounce of concern, even after all he now knew. Receiving an "I'm sorry," would be just too much to ask, he realized, and for once Tony should just stop trying to get it. It would only ring hollow and empty and do little to change their present, anyway.

He tried to refocus his attention. "I'll see to your wishes, I'll get it all done, but know this: your life has cost me, and your other children, however many there are, so much pain."

Tony let go of his father's hand. Either his or his father's hand grew slicker with sweat, he wasn't sure which. He wiped his palm on his pant leg and stood up, waiting for his father's answer, but none came. His speech, and particularly the questions about the legitimacy of his business ventures, had apparently fallen on deaf ears. There were a number of rumors, as well as queries he hadn't answered, piled up in the office. Tony didn't know who to trust beyond Allen to help him straighten them out.

Never mind the business. He could pay the debts and the lawyers, even a few lawsuits if they came, with the money from selling things off. Wouldn't that have seemed suspicious in and of itself? He didn't care, answering his own thoughts, so long as he and Jina came out unscathed. He almost lost his whole life, dragged by the man before him and all his associates. Though it weighed on him, a certain final subject hadn't been spoken.

"About Sheila... is that your child?" he asked.

"I'm not - I'm not sure..." His father tried to turn his head away, but he could only move it so much. His body seemed stiff from the neck down. He didn't have to move at all: Tony saw the resignation on his face without the need for any words or body language. It was all evident - the silence told more than words could ever express.

Tony rolled his eyes, wondering if anyone would claim this poor child.

"She can burn in hell," his father spat. "We can find out the paternity easily but it doesn't matter, she's not fit to rear children. She must go to jail, for this." Alex tried to gesture with his chin to his present state, laying out before them.

"She'll get nothing, nothing. Find - find the paternity and if it's... if it's mine, can you please, please, take my child from her? The baby will be your sibling, son, if it's mine, but I can't be sure. It would give me peace if you, and Jina would take him or her, son? Would you do that for me, please?"

25

"I know it's a lot," his father went on. "I have no right to ask, but I'll give you more money for doing this. They can have a chance with you and..."

"Stop it." It was all Tony could think to say right then. His father wasn't even worthy of uttering his wife's name, let alone asking him something so out of the blue. The question occurred to him of whether his father really was of sound mind after all, or if he had lost some of it.

The man before him was clearly crazy - how else could he reconcile asking Tony the things he did? Maybe he hadn't heard the story of the last ten minutes, Tony thought. Then again, maybe he'd heard all of it, understood it, and still simply didn't care. That was Alex King's modus operandi. He'd listed off the things he wanted Tony to do but nothing more, only monetary compensation. *Just clean up the mess and try to move on with life, take my money as payment for your irreparable heartbreak, a litany of resentful children and broken homes and families.* As if money was better than apology, remorse, or public acknowledgement of paternity. Nothing else in Alex King's warped mind trumped money's ability to fix the things he'd done. He would just exit this life soon enough, leaving Tony, and the rest of his children, to deal with the fallout.

All the resentment - that up until now had been vying with feelings of care for a man at an end of his own making - quickly dissipated, leaving in their place a kind of hate that he knew could consume him if he didn't get it in check. With this last request, that hatred came pummeling back to him full throttle. He had been holding on to it for years and now there it was, crystal clear and threatening to remove all the empathy he had for his father, whose terrible ways had infiltrated his life and nearly cost him everything. And, to make matters worse, his father had no clue.

"There's one more thing, uh, Keith - Keith Munrow."

Tony's heart sunk at the name.

"Tell him I'm sorry. I shouldn't have..." His father started to wheeze and cough uncontrollably. The nurse rushed forward, grabbing the cup on the tray table and offering it to him. She bent the white flexible straw, pushing it into his mouth as he struggled. The man gulped raggedly before resting again.

"I think he uh, he needs a little rest," suggested the nurse. "You're here, and he - he was very excited to see you." She nodded at Tony. "If you can maybe give him a half hour, I'm gonna change some things in here and see about his lunch, but then you guys come on back, okay?" She smiled and Tony nodded. He didn't want to come back at all, but he heard the wheezing of his father's labored breathing as he turned to the exit. Jina grabbed his arm as he came out more fully into the waiting area, but she didn't say anything. They moved further away in the next room to the couch, flanked by floor to ceiling window views of the city. Allen was there too.

"Did you make a note of all the things your father wanted - do they seem amicable to you?" Allen began, once they were closer to where he had a number of papers spread out before him.

"Yes, almost. Just – uh…" Tony stammered.

"I'll get you some coffee?" Jina offered and Tony was grateful. He hated that she was being so kind and agreeable, even though he shouldn't hide what his father asked. He vowed to tell her later, when they got home.

"Look, Tony," Allen said as soon as Jina left them. "I realize what he asked - the final part of it – was… a lot."

Tony scanned the large room, doing a cursory panoramic view of the place. He listened as Allen spoke levelly to him. The bright room in which they stood contrasted with his father's darkened quarters, with the quiet ethereal feel of death hovering around him, as if waiting to pounce. This spacious area had a smaller suite with a large oak table, a conference speakerphone sat in the middle of the large oval table. It all felt so hollow and institutional. This wasn't what he had envisioned when his father would come to, but this was his reality.

He folded his arms as he stared passed Allen. So this was where the rich got sick, tried to get well or, succumbed to their injuries. Their affairs still had to be handled, he supposed, even in the midst of all that. Something felt so wrong and hands-off about all the stuff around him. Even the security detail were present, near the door when they'd first entered, checking everyone in and out as they guarded his father: two muscled men like the ones Tony had encountered the day he'd visited his father. What a way to live your life. It repulsed him.

In the full kitchen at the other end of the area, Tony watched Jina fix him coffee at the counter. He prayed this wasn't how he would end when his own time came. A bunch of hired folks around to do your bidding. If they wanted something from you - to do you in, for instance… why did his father trust him, even? He quickly thought about Jina's father then: the entire family gathered at the modest colonial-style home, the bed at the Jameson family home, moved down to the living room by Dean, to ensure his father didn't have to navigate the stairs. Those were a considerate, thoughtful bunch of faith-and-kindness driven folks. Tony wasn't sure why the various contrasts suddenly stood out for him so starkly. Probably because his old man and Jina's had very different lives. They told stories about Mr. Jameson senior. He was a good man, not wealthy but with something better than wealth, as far as Tony was concerned. Plus, no one had been out to kill him and to help accelerate his already declining health.

Alex King could perhaps have had his children surround him like that, if he'd taken the time to acknowledge them all instead of dropping his seed in various willing women and promptly skipping town. He couldn't even be sure anyone loved him for him, or just for his money.

Tony took a deep breath and swung his eyes back to Allen, who stood expectantly. Tony tugged at the shirt he was wearing, feeling claustrophobic from the stale air, the smell of antiseptic and hand sanitizer. The button of his shirt was already undone, but he still could not get relief. He left it alone.

"Yes, it's a lot," he responded finally. "Rather than my family and I taking on yet one more thing, one more King family reject, I expect you should find a genealogy company to get everyone's cheek swabbed, spit in a cup, cut off a lock of hair, or whatever it is they do for this stuff. See if they will take this latest offspring, Allen, cause I'm not the one - I'm not. I just... can't," Tony said with finality. He knew he was trying to convince himself more than anyone.

"Think of the child," Allen pleaded, his voice an urgent whisper. Tony looked at him. He wouldn't be guilt-tripped by anyone, least of all someone on payroll who, if Tony hadn't called, would have continued to take the hefty retainer money while asking zero questions about his father's wellbeing.

"I was a child," Tony snapped at Allen. "I made it, and so will... *it*." He calmed when Jina looked back at him, his harsh whisper traveling across the room.

"Hey, uh," She said when she walked back over to them. She pushed Tony to the couch where they both sat down. "I know your dad must have said something intense, but I didn't catch all of it, his voice is not strong. Here," she handed him the coffee.

Tony shrugged, accepting the warm cup as he contemplated his father's latest utterings, coupled with the reminder from Allen. He was glad that she hadn't heard, he told himself, because it wasn't his problem. He tried to offer a smile at Jina, but they both knew it came out tight and strained.

"He said that, uh, uh… for us to find the rest of his children. He thinks there may be… ten. And he, uh, wants to give up the company, liquidate its assets and give some to charities, the rest in a fund to be distributed equally among all his children."

"Wow, that's something. Are they all older?" Jina questioned.

Tony almost choked on the hot liquid. He shook his head dismally before speaking. "There may be some... toddlers, even." *One not even yet born,* he thought to himself.

"Wow. Do you think the child Sheila is carrying is really his? They say you men can produce into your nineties, but goodness."

Tony almost smiled, but he was too annoyed. "I do not care," he said sharply.

"Don't say that," Jina admonished.

Tony shrugged.

"What charities does he want to leave money to? That means something, honey, he's trying to still do something good."

"My Mom's, uh, my mom's school."

"Howard? Oh honey, that's wonderful! She barely finished, so hopefully that will help someone else. Maybe a portion of it could go to expectant mothers trying to finish school, for childcare or something."

"Yeah," Tony agreed noncommittally.

"Look at me," Jina said.

Tony didn't flinch. So stuck in his own anger, he was trying really hard not to show the burgeoning rage that he didn't want to consume him.

"I know you're mad, look at me."

"Really?" Tony said flippantly. He swung his eyes to meet hers, before looking away again. Annoyed by the tears, he set his cup aside to wipe them. Angry tears, he maintained: he was just angry.

"Yes, I know. I feel your blood boiling through my touch on your arm."

Tony looked down at her fingers.

"He's asking you to clean up his affairs," she offered.

"Mess," Tony said, quickly correcting her niceties. Those should be reserved for someone who deserved them, and Alex King wasn't one of them.

"I know. He wrecked the lives of others and now he's on his deathbed, about to exit," Jina said. "He wants to do right by everyone, including you and your Mother. He doesn't have to want that. He could have asked to be buried with his money, or have a lavish funeral, not give a care about where it's all going. This shows that he wants to clean it up too, do whatever he can to give his children a future, at least the means for it, for their mothers - even if he's not a part of that. I'm certain he regrets everything."

Tony wondered if that was all true. He had heard the apologies, but what gave his father the audacity to ask him to help with that one last thing? It just seemed absolutely crazy to him. If Sheila was guilty of poisoning him, she'd be unfit to parent. She could even go to jail as she should. He hated to think of the child, even as he rejected it all, but any responsibility to help the person who might be his sibling weighed on him heavily.

A commotion near the door of the suite caused both Tony

and Jina to look up, their conversation forgotten. When two men marched toward him, he stood up automatically, bracing himself for what could only be more bad news.

"Anthony King? We want to ask you some questions about the murder of Sheila King."

26

Against his better judgment, Tony let himself be separated from Jina: another mistake that he quickly regretted. Holed up at the police station, with Allen present as his lawyer, he had some questions of his own.

"Mr. King, do you remember reaching out to one of our Detectives just a week before your accident?

"No," Tony answered. "As you know, my memory is gone as a result of the accident, for more than year, I'm not sure how long exactly. That is to say, I don't remember the accident, or a year leading up to it."

"Well, it seems you contacted us because you thought some shady business practices were going on at your father's company."

"Then that must have been what I thought. Hey, what does this have to do with the murder of his wife?"

The detective regarded him neutrally. "Were you trying to hide something by killing her?"

Tony's temper flared. "I didn't kill her. I stand to gain nothing. As sorry as I am to hear about whatever happened to her, I do not have anything to hide."

"The child she was carrying wasn't yours?"

"No, I thought... no, she tried to make me believe it was mine. I actually wrote something to myself and started to document the crazy things at my father's company. I have a letter I wrote that I can send you."

"Is this the letter you're talking about?"

Tony looked at the letter that was handed to him across the table. He snatched it, read it quickly and shook his head before rereading it a second time. The letter started out as his, the first paragraph only - but the letter they had said he drove his car into the tree purposely, in order to spare Jina the pain of knowing what he'd done and his infidelity.

"No, no." He stood up abruptly. "This isn't true. This isn't. I didn't write this." He searched his phone and found a copy of the letter he had really sent Jina, shoving it at them.

Allen spoke up. "Provide us a copy please, and we will have our own analysis done."

"Yes, yes." Tony felt sweat bead his forehead as he began to pace. "Someone is trying to separate me from my wife. I need to go there. I gotta go. Give me my phone..."

"We need a copy of this letter. We'll need to get your phone records to check the date of this."

"Fine, fine, do whatever you want. I have nothing to hide. I need make sure my wife is all right."

"Why would someone be after your wife?"

"What? Because there are crazy people in this world. My wife is the only thing I care about, now can I go?" Tony leaned his arms on the table. "Someone assaulted my wife years ago, that person was never found. Then, just a little over a week ago, someone yanked the stroller with my child in it right out of her hands, scaring my wife and pushing my son into an alley before taking off. I have no reports on that. For all the answers you do not have, I have even more. You're doing nothing but barking up my tree, while the real people are out there committing more crimes then you will ever solve."

"What do you know about Keith Munrow?"

"What?" Tony was nonplussed. "We were friends, but we're not anymore. I hired him as a favor to work at my father's company shortly after my father put me in charge."

"Do you know if he and Sheila were lovers?"

"What? No, I..." Tony trailed off. "My father said something about him, though - to tell Keith he was sorry for something - but then he went into a coughing fit and he didn't tell me... Allen, do you know what he was talking about?"

Tony tried to keep his voice level. In all the confusion about Sheila's baby with... whomever, he hadn't further thought about his father's mention of Keith at all.

"What is it, Allen?" Tony demanded, noticing an uncomfortable look on his lawyer's face.

Allen's eyes met his own. "Alex is Keith's father too, Tony. You are brothers."

Tony stepped back as if he'd just been struck. Long moments passed, as something clicked in his mind.

"It's his," he breathed. "The baby - the baby is Keith's baby, and that's why he killed her. That's it. The two of them would have killed me somehow, too - in that stupid car, like they tried to. They wanted the company and all the money, that's it. I'm in the way." He loudly clapped his hands together piercing the room. "I gotta go, now. Let me out of here." He pounded the military-green metal table, feeling ready to tear the place down.

The officer finally stood as Allen spoke.

"Do you have any reason to hold Mr. King? - do you have a warrant? Are you going to arrest him?"

The detective shook his head and opened the door to the interrogation room, with a blast of cool air. "Reopen my wife's case," Tony said hastily as he backed away. "I want that son of a bitch put away. It's him, I know it's him." He grabbed his phone from the table and left.

* * *

JINA WAS HOME, but she was not happy about it. In the kitchen, after giving up on attempting to clean or fix something for lunch, she instead paced the tiny space, waiting for Chyna and Dean to bring Robby back. That was the only reason she'd agreed to come straight home: to meet them. Otherwise she would have gone with Tony to do the stupidest thing of talking with the police. Him agreeing to it had made her so mad. They had no proof; Tony was just too nice. He had Allen with him, at least. While she didn't know Allen all that well, knowing Tony was there with an ally was of some comfort. She knew Tony didn't have anything to hide - *he knew that and Allen knew that, so why all this questioning*, she asked the air, annoyed. She just had to see Tony's face, then all would be well.

Despite the relief that they would all be together once again, Jina desperately wanted to know what had happened to Sheila and her unborn child. Everything happened so fast, she hadn't had time to consider that ultimately a life had been tragically lost. Two lives, she amended in horror. She was so sad for the child. Who on earth would do that?

Jina cradled her own belly, trying to push away such devastating thoughts. She had hated the woman: she was after her husband, after all, and judging by Tony's letter, she'd almost won out. But for her to die was too much. Perhaps she'd made a mistake with some other man. Jina tried hard to put it all out of her mind. Mourning that loss wasn't her grief to bear. Whatever else Sheila was, she'd been about to become a mother, and that meant something to her - at least, it should have.

The phone's unexpected trill pierced the air and her thoughts. Taking a deep breath, she grabbed it frantically from the table in hopes that it was Tony. "Dean," she said in greeting, trying to sound calm, but the pitch of her voice likely gave her away.

"Hey, what is going on? The news..."

Wherever he was - the airport, she assumed - was noisy, but hearing her son's babbling in the background eased her fearful heart just a little. It had only been twenty-four hours, but it felt like a lifetime since she'd held him in her arms.

"Oh, that? He - Tony's being questioned." She didn't watch the news much anymore, but she tried to scan the headlines.

"And your father-in-law's wife is dead – is that true?" Dean asked incredulously.

Jina nodded, but her pacing resumed with the tone of his voice. "Yes, that's what we heard – but Dean, don't start. You know that he had nothing to do with that."

She didn't actually believe her brother would seriously suggest that Tony had any involvement, but now was not the time to even joke or imply that he was capable of murder. Dean was as bad as Jojo, in the latter's absence, and it really worked her last nerve. Tony had messed up, and her brothers would do best to just stay out of her marriage. She knew their motivation was based in love and care, but it didn't get them into her good graces. Family was everything to her, and Tony and Robby were hers.

"Jina?"

"Don't Jina me," she snapped. "Tony was with me all night, Dean. Listen, you're way out of line. When are you guys getting here with Robby, anyway?"

"You know that's not what I'm saying," Dean defended.

"What are you saying, then?" she returned. It was too late: she felt that he had implied plenty.

"Okay, Jina - I'm just saying I'm concerned, is all. Are you alone?"

"Yes, but Tony will be here any moment."

"What about that Keith guy? Where is he?"

"Keith, Keith Munrow? What about him, what does he have to do with anything?" Jina got a sinking feeling in the pit of her stomach. She tried to put her anger away, listening more intently: she'd clearly missed something.

"Jina, listen, news reports are saying that Keith and Tony are supposedly brothers," Dean said.

Jina stopped pacing as she dropped the phone to the floor with a clatter. As she reached for it, the door burst open and the man in question stood before her.

27

"Dean, call the..." Jina yelled, hoping Dean could hear her. She couldn't finish her sentence before Keith grabbed her, stomping the phone into pieces as he did so.

The new information from Dean tumbled through her mind. *Was he a killer?* was her first thought. She didn't want to believe it, but her concern increased. He certainly wasn't there to bake cookies for Robby's homecoming. She thanked God her child wasn't there right at that moment. She'd let her guard down because she'd been with Tony for a while now, and she felt completely safe with him.

She tried to run to the back of the apartment, but barely reached the living room before Keith dragged her to the floor. He straddled her, pinning her arms to her side and preventing her from squirming. His legs squeezed, and she stopped fighting.

"Is this hot to you?" she gasped out, trying to inch herself out from under him. The more she did, however, the tighter his grip became.

Before she saw it coming, he landed a sound smack against her cheek and she felt her own teeth cut the inside. It stung.

She stilled her movements, fully aware and focused on him, as her cheek throbbed.

"Good, I see that I have your attention. And finally, babe, look - we're alone."

Keith breathed hard as if he'd been running a marathon. Stunned into silence, she looked at his eyes. The suit he wore - usually fresh pressed, pristine and wrinkle-free - was now dirty, a piece tattered at his neckline, ripped through to his skin, a part of his sleeve hanging loosely at the cuff. He heaved her up into a sitting position and backed away, sliding his gun out of his belt to brandish it in her face.

"You still got some smart things to say, huh? You can talk to my little friend here if you'd like."

Jina watched the gun silently before refocusing on him.

"Great - I see I have to result to more drastic persuasion."

"What do you want?" Jina leaned back against the sofa, drawing her knees up.

"What do I want?" Keith echoed. "Oh, how nice. Finally someone gives a damn about what I want."

"I don't," Jina replied coldly. "I'm just seeing what it is you think you can get here. Whatever it is, I'm pretty sure it's not here."

"Honey, you are just so full of niceties, aren't you? But what do I want? Oh, hmm, let's see... I want a million dollars."

"You could have had that. You could have gotten money from your rich father, now that he's on his deathbed."

"I could have gotten a lot of things, but he's so hell-bent on making your stupid husband King, pun intended, of everything, I wasn't good enough. When I found out, I even asked him for a job, and he didn't see fit to give me nothing. Then Johnny-come-lately shows up and he gets the world. Don't that beat all?"

"And that just burns you up, doesn't it?" Jina offered.

"Hell yeah," Keith snarled. "You know what else burns me up is stupid women with mouths, like you and Sheila. You just don't learn."

"So you killed her, and instead of a million dollars, you'll have a pretty little jail cell - and for what? For nothing?" Jina tried to keep the emotion out of her voice as she thought about the woman that wrecked her life. She hadn't deserved to die over it.

"Maybe. I'm just so sick and tired of these women," Keith said, before letting out a laugh.

"I'm sure they're sick and tired of you too." Jina replied. She resisted the urge to rub her face even as it burned: she wouldn't give him the satisfaction. Her retorts likely didn't help her cause, but it wasn't like her to go quietly. She was angry. She'd had her family right there in her grasp, she considered in frustrated desperation: finally, the pieces had found a solid foundation. Now she found that the man before her had been trying to unravel and tear it apart all along. She couldn't believe she hadn't suspected him.

Keith laughed at Jina again, and she just stared at him. "Man, you always had that mouth," he murmured. "Your mouth gonna get you killed, Jina Jameson King. You're in no position to be so ugly."

"And you're a walking dead man," she retorted. "You're going to go to jail for a long time for whatever you've done. It's probably a much longer list of offenses than Tony or I could have ever imagined about you."

"Oh, you have no idea, sweetheart," replied Keith. "You want to know about my very first crime? - after the bit of petty theft in my teens of course, that was nothing. Lookee here. Does this look familiar to you?"

Jina watched as he pulled a necklace from his pocket. A bit tarnished twenty years later, it still caught the bright sunlight as it twirled before her eyes: the necklace that had been ripped from her neck the night of her assault. Her very first gift from

Tony. She had been devastated to lose that one: it wasn't worth any money, but its sentimental value for her and Tony couldn't be replaced. He'd searched to find her another one just like it, but he couldn't.

She swallowed hard, trying not to let the emotion in her voice come through. "So you caught me unawares," she responded, trying to remain nonchalant. "And here you are, still sneaking up on women that don't like you. You're a disgusting loser that nobody likes, copping a feel in the dark because no one would dare let you touch them in the broad daylight."

"Shut up, shut up!" He was on her again, grabbing the lapels of her shirt, yanking her toward him. He put the gun to her head, but he didn't pull the trigger. She felt it push into her temple, but she stared him down, trying a different approach."Just tell me why?" she managed, and immediately felt his grip loosen.

He pushed her roughly away before backing up to the chairs across from her with a harsh laugh. "Why? Because I had a plan - but you and Sheila kept ruining everything I worked so hard for."

"What did you work hard for?" She tried to sound engaged. She read too many police reports and too many news stories not to know how self-absorbed and narcissistic so many criminals were. They always wanted engagement and, as sad as it was, a listening ear and a few questions to indulge their ramblings. It was simply something she came to learn over the course of her career in journalism. She knew that often, such patient listening got to the heart of their anger and resentment – and that it could extend her time to wait for her husband or Dean and Chyna. She cringed at the latter, knowing she had to do something. Thankfully, Chyna and Dean didn't have a key to their place, but...

Jina chanced a glance at the door, which she could see from her vantage point. It was cracked only a sliver, and the chain dangled, broken. Perhaps that would concern them, warning them not to enter at all. She hoped fervently that he'd heard her on the phone. Her prayers increased for a solid plan to avoid the worst possible ending.

She focused on Munrow, nodding as he spoke, to indicate interest where she had zero. She tried to come up with more ways to engage him, even as she listened with half a disgusted ear to the extent of his crimes.

"I worked to be recognized for my real estate picks in the last year," he went on. "Before he got really ill, I advised Mr. King on the real estate he should buy. I would pass all this on to Tony when he first hired me. They were all good investments - but he didn't pay me any attention. He just wanted to manage everything, keep it flowing until his father returned. Stupid idiot: little did he know that his father wasn't going to return, washed up old man." Keith sniffed derisively. "Tony gave me some nothing job, just helping out with the books. Well, in the end I helped myself to the books."

"So how much did you get? Why not be happy with that?"

"You're so good, Madam Journalist." Keith laughed again. "Gonna write a book about me? A thriller? That might be cool actually. Give me a cool name, okay?"

"You can write it yourself, in prison," she retorted.

"Oh, good one," Keith snorted.

"I don't see any good in this," she replied seriously. "The authorities are going to find out you killed Sheila. How is she even involved?"

"Oh man," he said coldly, shrugging. "That woman is – was - something else. She lied about the paternity of that baby she was carrying. I don't want no baby, and if it was Tony's, now he can't have it either."

"It's not his. He didn't cheat on me."

"Yeah, I figured he didn't, goodie two shoes. It was fun seeing him having those little deer-caught-in-the-headlights moments when he thought he had, though. Woo woo, I cheated on my wife, oh my God... Not to mention the rift. The more he thought he was losing you, the more he focused on work. He finally wanted to do something with the company. Sheila and I had a good laugh about that, that's for sure."

Jina felt sick. "The child could have been given up for adoption. You didn't have to do... that, when you don't even know the truth of the baby's paternity." Her heart hurt from all he said.

"Well, what if it was mine? She gives it up for adoption, only to somehow be finding me in eighteen years? No thanks," he said disgustedly.

Jina looked away. His ability to imagine the future child coming for him some day both confused and saddened her. He had no feeling whatsoever for what he'd done: he couldn't see the consequences from his own actions. He couldn't take himself out of the equation enough to let the child live regardless. No one could make him take that responsibility. So many fathers hadn't, including his before him. It was clear how much Alex King's rejection stung him. Keith Munrow was afraid of an adult child finding him: perhaps a conscience, however misguided, did exist inside him somewhere.

"So why assault me?" she asked.

"Oh, hmm, what can I say, that was personal," Keith returned. "You're always in my damn way. Tony threw a fight just so he could go out with you. Isn't that stupid? I had ten G's on that fight and I lost it! How dare he give up on something I had money riding on? He had no right. You could have waited."

"Did he know you were betting on his fights?" Jina asked. She remembered that date with Tony. She'd nursed his swollen eyes, his cut lip and begged him to give up what she couldn't see as a career.

"Why would I tell him that?" Keith said in exasperation. "He didn't have to throw it - he could have had money too, ya know? I told him we could do twenty Gs and I'd give him some on top of the prize money he was already gonna get. I was the brains, every time I was involved in something, I helped him, and I got nothing in return. No, instead he left me high and dry, explaining why he threw the fight when he could have won so easily. Who does that? I got a pretty good beat down for that: I didn't have the money. Then you talked him into quitting fighting altogether, got him into school - you're a regular Iyanla Vanzant, aren't you, fixing up his life when his life was fine as it was. He was good! He might just have been a local name, but I was working to change that. He could have been a legend, he could have rivaled Mike Tyson even. Instead you got him being some executive in his father's company, pushing paper and visiting properties and lobbying with bigwigs. He didn't need you to do nothing, but you stuck your nose in our business anyway."

"I didn't want him to work for his father's company," Jina corrected him. "I told him to forgive his father, not clean up his stupid mess, and I certainly didn't tell him to hire you and give you a chance. I did feel sorry for you, though, and so did he. You grew greedy, but his intentions, his heart and all of his motivations were honest. We can't say the same for you, now can we?"

"Ah, but I'm smart, I made something out of nothing. Tony hired me because he felt insecure. Your big strong husband couldn't make it as an executive: he needed my help, so I helped. We had something before you. I was making him into something. The only thing he felt from you was pressure. We had a good thing going. We were brothers, and we could have been millionaires by now. I hated you for that. So yes, it was me. I loved watching how skittish you became afterwards - afraid of life, afraid of your shadow, barely leaving your precious off-campus apartment, afraid of the damn dark."

His face clouded. "I still hate you. You interrupted my

plans, you and Sheila. You're still interrupting our relationship."

With that he stood up and moved toward her menacingly. Just then, the door swung open again, causing Keith to turn in surprise. Jina managed to scramble up and grab the remote on the coffee table, the only thing she could find. She smashed it against Keith's head, where a small gash appeared. Keith grunted, but it didn't knock him out. In the moments that he staggered from the blow, she yelled for Tony.

"He has a gun!" Suddenly she couldn't see anything: she squeezed her eyes shut as a blinding pain shot through her stomach, and she collapsed. From the floor, she watched blearily as the two men struggled. It felt as if she were having an out of body experience. She heard punches and yelling, and she thought she heard the police and Dean's voice - then a shot rang out.

28

Once Keith was down, Tony stood back as the police rushed in. He glanced down at the other man's wounds, which from what he could see weren't fatal. As he backed away, he touched his own body, his chest, his neck and face, disbelieving that he'd come out with zero injuries. He'd been on Keith for all of twenty seconds when he saw Jina fall down as they struggled. When he got over to her and turned her face toward his, he noticed that she had a small red print on her cheek, and his teeth ground. "Jina, Jina, talk to me."

She looked at him, focusing her eyes. He could see that she questioned him, though she said nothing at all. She was searching his face as she reached up to touch him. He held her hand, gripping it like a lifeline. "Jina, is it the baby? Did he hurt you? Please tell me." Tony's voice caught in his throat. "I need an ambulance. I need help," he yelled to the paramedics. "She's pregnant," he added.

"All right, let's get her up to the hospital - we will do it, sir, please stand back."

Tony cradled her ready to lift her, but they prevented him from doing anything, even from touching her, as they fetched an uncomfortable-looking stretcher. He followed them out of the building, where Dean rushed up to them.

"What the hell did you do? This is my sister... what is going on here?" he said quickly, assessing the situation.

"We're not sure, but she's complaining of abdominal pain - we'll know soon," replied one of the paramedics as they hurried past. "We're going to have to take her to INova, we have a smaller bus, you'll need to meet us there. Sir, can you please see to it that Mr. King gets there safely?"

"Yes," Dean said quickly. "We can take my car."

Tony nodded: he couldn't argue. As much as he hated being separated from Jina, maybe they could beat her there. He'd use the time to pray, while he urged Dean to drive as fast as he could.

* * *

TWENTY-FOUR HOURS PASSED QUICKLY, and Tony ran through every emotion: anger, fear, sadness, a kind of grief at the unknown, and then, when he saw his wife at last, disbelief, followed finally by joy that Jina and his unborn child were safe. The stress of everything took a toll, and Jina was not only dehydrated, she needed immediate bed rest for the foreseeable future, but her and baby would be fine.

He sat up in the chair that had been his bed and his holding cell for the last day and a half, watching his wife sleep. She could sleep for six more months if she wanted, so long as she followed the routine of eating, letting him escort her to the bathroom, then stay awake long enough for them to have deep conversations about everything, until she drifted off to sleep again. The last time he was up, Chyna and Dean had brought Robby and they'd had a nice visit.

He wanted to go and get the boy now, just so Jina could be with him again. It was time to get on with their lives. Tony hadn't showered in three days, and he had no plans to do so until Jina was coming home.

"What are you thinking about?"

"You, of course - you're all I think about." Tony smiled when she spoke. He stood and stretched before sitting gingerly upon the bed. He leaned in, bracing his hands on either side of her shoulders and kissing her. "Good morning."

"Hey, good morning," Jina smiled.

"I uh, got this cleaned." Tony held out the necklace to her. Though she smiled, she started to cry. Gently, he pulled her into his arms, soothing her, feeling partly responsible for it all.

"It's like it's brand new," she said admiring the piece through the tears. "I thought it was fake?"

"No fake stuff for my girl. It's real," Tony said in mock offense.

"But how could you afford that, back then?"

Tony grinned. "I saved up the money from three of my fights. Trust me, it's legit." He put the necklace on, holding her head and fixing it so it hung just right as he eased her back into the pillow. "I told you it was fake so you would be less devastated when that deranged criminal took it. But no fake stuff for my real girl. Never."

Jina touched it against her chest. "I love it."

"I love you." Tony replied, running his finger across the charms of the necklace and touching her chest.

"I have a question."

"Nothing too serious, but go ahead." Tony replied.

"Did you feel pressured to make money for us when you took your father's company?"

Tony shrugged.

"Tell the truth," she pressed. "Keith said,"

"Who?" he asked sharply. "That man's name has no business being uttered by your lips. His gunshot wound is fine; he's already in jail where he belongs."

"Just hear me out," Jina persisted. "I still want to know if what he said was true - if you took the position out of ..."

"Out of some blind hope that that he, Alex-the-terrible-King, would value me, love me even? No. I had a job - it didn't make much, but it was honest and it was enough for us. I would do whatever I could for you and Robby and this one we got cooking right here." He patted her belly tenderly. "My father and that Keith Munrow can both go to hell."

"How is your father doing?" Jina asked.

Tony hung his head. "He was lucid long enough for the judge to declare him competent to change his will, long enough for him to turn it over to me. Allen was able to secure that, at least. The rest is for me to figure out. I just need to execute his wishes and be done. I haven't seen him since the day we were there together, but he's not talking well. His paralysis can't be reversed, and he can't swallow solid food."

"He might talk to you, you might put wind in his sails," Jina suggested. "He may be sad that you haven't come by."

"You know, everyone thinks you're this tough old, flippant, mouthy, harsh-comeback, get-you-told-before-your-coffee-gets-cold wife o' mine, but if they only knew your heart is the softest I've ever seen. Even after everything, Jina."

"It keeps everyone on their toes," she smiled. "Only you can know my secrets, and the real me. When can we get out of here, anyway? This pregnant woman has needs, you know; and I gotta call Momma, let her know I'm all right."

"Do you now? Oh, I like that, the lady and her needs part. That family stuff obviously ain't for everybody." They laughed and he hugged her, going in for another kiss.

There was a knock on the door. "Do you want visitors? I can get rid of them," Tony whispered as he kissed her cheek.

"It's fine, let's see," Jina smiled. She pushed the button to raise the hospital bed into a sitting position, while he moved to the door to greet whoever it was.

It was Allen. This was the first time Tony had seen him in

anything other than a pristine three-piece suit. Today's attire looked like he might have been out driving his favorite sports car instead of litigating Alex King's affairs. "Uh, good morning - glad to hear you're doing better, Jina."

"Thank you, Allen."

"Tony."

Tony nodded his greeting but otherwise didn't speak. He and Allen were still cordial, but Tony remained annoyed about the fact that Allen hadn't informed him more about Keith when his father had told him, several years ago. It could have solved a lot. He knew there was lawyer-client confidentiality and all that, but it was his life on the line, and that particular point of recent contention strained whatever growth their relationship might have had. He wanted to trust the man with his father's affairs as well as his own, but considering everything, it would take time. His father obviously trusted the wrong people, and Tony didn't want to go down that same road. As soon as he wrapped up his father's affairs, his estate and his eventual funeral, Tony would have nothing else to do with any of it. That was a promise he would maintain.

Tony held out his hand to the side, waiting expectantly for Allen to speak. "Something I need to review and sign, what is it? Is Alex dead?"

"Tony!" Jina whispered reprovingly, but Allen didn't flinch. Tony eyed Allen a little more closely. As unflappable as the lawyer usually seemed, today he saw that even Allen looked uncomfortable.

"So, just some new developments that I've been alerted of," he began. There was a pause. "Sheila's baby was delivered this morning, by emergency Caesarean."

29

"There are some decisions to be made," Allen continued.

"They aren't any more decisions that haven't already been made by me. I informed you of what we were going to be doing," Tony replied sternly.

"She survived?" Jina questioned, a hand on her heart. She couldn't believe what she was hearing.

Allen looked over at Jina. "Not really. She is brain dead - Sheila is, to clarify. Keith had enough mercy to report a suspected attack, and the ambulance got to her to render aid; but she also hit her head - or he hit her - and that caused a Traumatic Brain Injury. They kept her alive artificially, long enough to give the baby just a little more time, but a decision was made that the baby seemed healthy and should be delivered." He let out a long breath. "Did you know she'd survived?"

"No, no," Tony defended.

"No, Tony didn't know, but before..."

"You know, what are you even doing here?" Tony cut in. "I said what I said."

"Tony, that was what your father asked," Jina went on. "For you to take Sheila's baby?"

"Yes, before we knew Sheila was killed or injured, that's what my Father asked me to do," snapped Tony.

"How long do we have to decide?" Jina directed her question to Allen.

"Jina you're not serious?" Tony cried, as he turned to her. He hated that Allen had brought this to her: he likely knew what he was doing when he did so.

"My wife does not need this stress, this headache, this nightmarish dream that will not leave us be," Tony continued. "It's time for you to leave."

"She'll go up for adoption," Allen offered.

"She?" Jina looked up.

"Yes, a girl. The baby's a girl," Allen offered.

"Stop it," Tony said sharply. "Leave, now." He took a threatening step toward Allen, who didn't budge.

"I am serious as a heart attack," Jina piped up. "I want us to think about this, Tony, just... let's talk. How long, Allen? Is there a next of kin on Sheila's side?"

Allen shook his head, "Not that we've found. We're doing a search, but it could take weeks, if not months."

"Jina, our lives are really complicated right now. Why are we even having this discussion?"

"Because I want to. Because it's important, it means something to me too. This isn't something you should have just said no to and been done. You may very well regret your actions in the future - not to mention the fact that it should mean something to you, too."

She looked toward the door as Allen left quietly, leaving her and Tony to have a conversation.

The silence echoed in her ears when Tony said nothing, however. As her heart ran, her mind also raced with so many thoughts. "I prayed for that child's soul just the other day. I barely had time to grieve her loss. Someone should grieve her, if not her own father, whoever that is. Through all of that, she survived. God saw fit to give her a fighting chance. Now she needs someone who will support her."

"You're asking a lot, Jina - the freakin' impossible if you ask me."

Jina was thoughtful. Although she felt she didn't have the strength she needed right then, she also felt God's hand in all of this. Slowly, her determination returned. All he had to do was to tell Allen no without considering her wishes. She could feel her heart crack at the thought. She tried to see the future. She knew she would wonder about this poor, innocent baby for the rest of her days, contemplating and speculating on the kind of life she would have.

"She's your sister, honey - does that not mean anything to you?" she continued.

"Ha, yes my sister, or, or hey, she's my niece? We don't even know now, do we?" Tony threw up his hands in exasperation. "Oh and by the way, she could be neither."

"She is something," Jina quietly reminded him. "She is *somebody*: a human being first and most of all. The only thing that matters is giving her a hope and a future, Tony. We could give her that."

Tony moved back to his wife's bed and took a deep breath as he sat down in the chair. He tried to keep his anger at bay. His wife was upright and talking, he reminded himself, and his unborn child was still safe inside. Regardless of what else happened, he had that, and he was thankful. He looked at Jina, waiting expectantly, and earnestly tried to understand her reasoning.

"Was that what your father was asking you the other day?" Jina pressed.

Tony nodded. "Calling it 'the other day' makes it seem like yesterday, though. What we've been through felt like about ten years."

"Don't change the subject," Jina warned.

He managed a smile at her and reached for her hand. "I know what you think."

He frowned when she withdrew her hands from his and stuck them under the covers.

"You don't know," she insisted.

"I do," Tony countered. "You think that maybe if something happens to your, our child, we should take this one. How dare we once have dreamed about having a house full of children, only for us to reject this little girl after we had so much trouble conceiving and building our family in these past few years? No, it's not like that. You have told me so many times that God doesn't function in some kind of barter economy. Do this, take this one, and I'll give you this shiny, object instead for your troubles. That's not how it works. This child, our child, will be fine. I'm just saying: this other one is not quite right for us."

"She's a gift," Jina whispered.

"Yes, Jina, to someone, but not us," Tony insisted.

"We'll take her," Jina announced.

Tony shook his head.

"You think you know so much about me and my feelings," she said. "But I know something about you, too. I know you carry resentment in your heart: about... her, and about your father."

"Whatever." Tony stood and looked out of the window. The pain of what Jina said struck him right in the heart.

"She wrecked my whole life - why shouldn't I feel resentment?" he returned over his shoulder. He couldn't deny it: Jina was right about his thoughts. He might never be capable of caring for this other child as much as he cared for his own biological children, and that scared him more than anything: more, even, than rejecting her outright. He believed what he said, even if what he said was all wrong; but all this baby represented would stare him in the face every single day. How could he love her through that?

"She didn't wreck your whole life. You are blessed," Jina continued, trying to talk some sense into him. "She doesn't know a single thing about you and she doesn't care about you, not right now. She could grow to care for you, though, when you show her what caring is - what love is."

"Well, hello everyone - here she is!"

A sing-song voice greeted Tony and Jina before they saw the person attached to it: a woman in colorful scrubs, pushing a wheeled cart into the room. The wheels' squeaky noise filled the room as she brought it close to Jina's bed. Jina was the first to peer over, and when she looked at Tony her eyes were filled with tears.

"What - what are you? What is she doing in here?" Tony was the first to chastise the nurse.

The woman looked taken aback. She looked back and forth between the two of them, eyebrows raised. Her hands went up to put her fingers against her forehead, clearly confused. "I thought… I heard she was your sister. She's so sweet, she has the King family eyes. She's gonna be so fortunate."

"No."

The nurse hesitated. Her uncertainty about what to do next was amply evident on her face: startled, confused and sad at the same time. She pulled the cart back, ready to return from whence she came; but Jina reached out hastily to pull the cart closer to her bed. The nurse lifted her hands in surrender.

"I'm sorry, I'm sorry," she began. "CPS is here with a lawyer - perhaps I made a mistake. I can take her."

"The lawyer - of course." Tony laughed.

"No, leave her - let's just have a visit?" Jina beseeched him.

"Oh, okay, that will be really nice. I'll just, uh, go."

The nurse hesitated, then hurried so fast from the room that Jina smiled at the sight of the poor woman scurrying away. The baby however, who had been quiet but alert and looking around, begin to wail unexpectedly.

"Pick her up," Jina barked: it was almost an order. The small pain in her side, her slightly protruding belly and the stupid safety railing all conspired to prevent her from getting the child herself. She almost got up on her knees, but Tony came closer when she threatened to do so. She pushed back the cover, kicking her legs free, effectively letting him know how serious she was.

"If I weren't in this stupid bed, I would seriously fight you right now, Tony, and knock some sense into you. Pick. Her. Up."

Tony looked. Admittedly he'd been curious, and some strange urge did draw him to the crib, but his arms remained by his sides. It was as if he warred inside to pick up the child, even as he maintained his erect body, fighting his own strong inclination to do as Jina ordered. After a long moment's pause, he found himself leaning in slowly, although he didn't reach for the child straight away.

The instinctual need to sooth her soon won out, however, and Tony reached down. He knew that when he did, it was all over. A girl, and a fatherless, motherless girl at that, would ruin anyone with half a heart.

His breathing labored, he picked her up, and as soon as she was situated more comfortably in his arms, her wailing ceased. Moving the crib to the side, Tony closed the distance between the two of them and Jina. With one hand, he managed to ease the railing down and sat heavily on the bed. His energy was completely drained by the inner war he'd just had with himself – or maybe with God.

"She's so pretty," Jina breathed. "We're gonna take her - we'll adopt her, and we'll love her as if she is one of our own. We can tell her someday about her parents, but first we will show her love. This is it, Tony: no more animosity, resentment, jealousy or evil. We can break this vicious cycle of all these fatherless children in your lineage – this cycle of everyone feeling somehow slighted, driven to viciousness, lust, envy, pride, greed, gluttony, violence..." Her breath caught. "And all that wrath, and even the slothfulness that prevented them from making their own way, their own money, and caused them to try to get ahead on the success of someone else. I bind these things in the name of Jesus."

Tony listened. His eyes closed but he felt her hand moving, touching his forehead. Her thumb wiped his tears and gently grazed the child's head, as she prayed for all of them. As odd as it seemed, Tony felt the constriction in his chest ease, his own anger and hatred gradually leaving him, as though a weight had been lifted.

When Jina opened her eyes, she stared at him and he leaned his forehead against her, kissing her. She wiped his tears away as they marveled together at the child.

"What's her name?"

Tony leaned back and shook his head. "I don't, I don't know."

"We will call her Truth," Jina offered.

"Truth? True King?" Tony echoed, testing it out. "Is that a little - ?" Tony laughed at her look, but the meaning of his wife's name for this child was not lost on him. He knew to leave well enough alone.

"Well, we'll need a nickname of some sort," he conceded. He understood what she was trying to do: to change the trajectory of the family. At that moment, he was so glad he'd married someone like her. She was the truth personified, really. He couldn't see his life without her, and he was glad he didn't have to.

Jina leaned in to kiss the baby and in spite of himself, Tony kissed her tiny forehead too.

"I think at this point in our marriage, I'm just along for the ride," he grinned.

"And the food," Jina added, "don't forget, better up your serving portions, we got lots of little mouths to feed now."

"Are we really doing this?" Tony smiled.

"I think you know what we're doing here, but it's good of you to ask. We can do this. I love you and I'll be with you through this. We're doing it together."

"You better, or all bets are off."

Not surprisingly, Allen returned with the paperwork, which he conveniently just happened to have in his weathered briefcase. There was information from CPS, the court orders for emergency guardianship and protections, as well as paperwork detailing what they would have to do next, including a court hearing to be set for another few months to make it all legal. They took turns holding the child, as Tony wondered just what he was in for. He looked forward with hope for the first time in months.

30

S *even Months Later...*

THE STATE of the room in their tiny apartment where Robby, True and Canton King, the newest addition, slept was as if a cyclone had hit it. It was late evening; the kids had just their bath and cuddle time with their dad and mom before being put down for the night. Jina looked around at all the clutter and wouldn't have it any other way. With so much energy still at this late hour, she tenderly fussed with a painting of seahorses and faeries that Chyna had painted for her children on one wall of the room. She hoped to add a few dreamy pieces, and soon the children's names in wood, too, when Chyna finished carving them.

Because he never slept anyway, Robby stood up now to watch her, and she laughed. "You're supposed to be sleeping," she whispered to him. The baby just smiled, shoving fingers in his mouth as he began to bounce up and down.

She struggled to put the picture up just right. Tony had

put it up, but she'd insisted on moving it to her liking while he took a shower. Even though she had been feeling fine lately, she was still sore and still moving very gingerly about everything - but she was upright and now determined to do everything.

"It's almost time for you to get a big boy bed, huh?" she whispered, when she'd finished with the picture.

She turned to admire her children. She sometimes even snuck into their room at odd hours of the night, often finding Robby up watching the two others, holding court over them, no doubt keeping the boogieman and other such scary things at bay. He was their personal protector, too - just like her own siblings, she supposed, had been growing up. She couldn't imagine not having this now, even though she never saw it all coming into her life.

Even Tony was a little different. He treated True so well. He was fast becoming a girl dad, and Jina loved watching the two of them together. She and he had both learned so much about each other, about family, sacrifice, real generosity, and love. She had everything she could have dreamed, only this was better, because it was real.

"What are you doing?" Tony came back into the room hurriedly. Since the difficult birth, and the last few months, he was rarely away from her side. He pulled her into his arms, and her stomach fluttered as it always did when he picked her up. He carried her two feet from the wall where the painting was and sat down in the chair with her on his lap.

"Nothing, I was just..." she began sheepishly.

"Doing too much, again," Tony admonished. "Come get your Mother, Robby. She's hardheaded," he said to the child, who played with a toy in his crib. His head popped up when his father mentioned his name, but he was otherwise uninterested in the two of them.

"Oh, come here, sexy Momma."

"Am I still sexy to you?" she giggled.

"Try me?"

"No," She smiled. "Wait your turn - it's not time for that yet."

"Well when it is, we're going to find out how sexy I think you truly are. And the next time you mess with that picture and use that stepstool for anything, you're going over my knee," he chided. "That sound sexy, too?"

"Depends on what happens after," she laughed.

"Don't tease me." Tony blushed, pulling her closer and rocking them both in the chair.

Jina smiled. "Mommy good, daddy bad."

"Bad daddy." Robby piped up, hitting his toy.

She laughed again. "I think that I won that round."

Tony shrugged. "You two can have each other, I have two other perfect little people that haven't learned to be prejudiced against me just yet."

"I'll still win." She said, nipping his ear lobe.

"I won," Tony said seriously. He stopped rocking to look at her. The room was dark, save for the two nightlights on either side of the room, but they could see each other perfectly.

"Thank you for being so firm about True," Tony said softly. "I would have regretted everything had it not been for you."

Jina smiled. "I know you would. I wouldn't let you make a bad decision if I could help it. I had to protect both our hearts."

Tony nodded. "A trial has been set for Keith's crimes," he added.

"I heard. What about your father's funeral?" Jina asked quietly.

"It's next week. All the families of his twelve children – the twelve they've identified so far, at least - have been notified. Some said they're coming, some not. But curiosity is probably what's driving them. I can't be sure."

"You need to forget about what they think or say to you

about any of it," Jina said firmly. "Tony, I also need you to brace yourself for the grief. I know you haven't even processed it yet, but I know it's gonna come. Every emotion, you just tell me when you feel it. I can handle it. Trust me, it's gonna hurt."

"I see that now," Tony agreed. "I didn't think I would, but I see it."

"I love you so much, Tony."

"I love you and I'm so thankful to you. Jina, I've been thinking. I want us to recommit to our vows this anniversary: to marry each other again."

It was then that Tony stood up, with Jina bundled in his arms. "What are you doing?"

He set her down on the floor, ensuring she had her balance before backing away from her. She watched him go down on one knee before her eyes. "You're serious?"

"Yes, very. Marry me, Jina, again?"

He pulled out a ring and grabbed her hand, sliding it on. It fit her current ring like a top piece, with a small cutout for the diamond and three different stones around the cutout, for each of her children's birth months. She brought it up to the light and admired it.

"It's beautiful, Tony."

Tony stood, pulling her close. Jina buried her face in his chest, sobbing as he picked her up and carried her to their room.

She must have stared at the ring until she fell asleep in her husband's arms, thinking about all the wonderful things she had: her husband, her family, security, safety and love – in other words, the only things that mattered.

THE END

DEAR READER

I hope you have enjoyed Tony and Jina's story. As always, I appreciate you choosing to spend time with my writing and the characters I create. Thank you so much for supporting my craft and me. I cannot begin to tell you how rewarding this endeavor has been. Send me a letter or email me at hello@traceegarner.com, visit my website and use the "Contact Tracee" form at www.traceegarner.com - and be sure to follow me on Instagram, Twitter and Facebook to see what's going on with my next projects. Jojo is finally coming, now that I've finished Jina's story. I have some awesome Reader's Guide questions on my website, so let me know your thoughts about this cast of characters, the Jameson's and the King's, the storyline, or whatever else you'd like to share. I look forward to hearing from you.

Don't forget, if you have time, please consider leaving a brief review on Amazon, Goodreads, Barnes and Noble or any other bookseller platform. I would appreciate it so much. Until next time, I wish you the best.

Tracee

ABOUT THE AUTHOR

Tracee Lydia Garner is a national best-selling and award-winning author. A Virginia native, she currently resides in the northern Virginia area with her family. She is an advocate for persons with disabilities and often speaks to people with disabilities, youth, minorities and women. She enjoys writing and cooking tremendously and, of course, loves to read. Tracee is a member of the Romance Writers of America.